I'll Love You When You're More Like Me

I'll Love You When You're More Like Me

M.E. Kerr

LIZZIE
SKURNICK
BOOKS

Brooklyn, New York

Printed in the United States
Reissue Edition
10 9 8 7 6 5 4 3 2 1

No part of this book may be used or reproduced in any manner
without written permission of the publisher.
Please direct inquiries to:
Lizzie Skurnick Books
an imprint of Ig Publishing
392 Clinton Avenue #1S
Brooklyn, NY 11238
www.igpub.com

ISBN: 978-1-939601-06-3 (paperback)

For Marcella Pardo and her sister, Renee—
to remember the East Hampton years.

1. Wallace Witherspoon, Jr.

One warm night in May, in the back of the hearse, while I was whispering "I love you, I love you," into Lauralei Rabinowitz' soft, black hair, she said, "Stop right there, Wally! There are three reasons this can't go on any longer!"

"*Three* reasons?" I said.

"Three reasons," she said, sitting up, reaching into her blazer pocket for her comb. She combed her hair while she told me what they were.

"One," she said, "you're not Jewish."

"Two," she said, "you're shorter than I am."

"And three," she said, "you're going to be an undertaker."

"You knew all that!" I complained.

"I know I knew all that," she said, "but I couldn't stop myself before. Now I'm stopping myself."

"You can't!" I insisted. "I'll probably want to marry you someday."

"I just did," said Lauralei Rabinowitz, "and I'd never marry you in a million years, Wally Witherspoon."

So much for ancient history. I am now unofficially engaged to Harriet Hren, who does want to marry me, isn't Jewish, and standing, even in heels, just reaches my shoulder.

Our plans to marry when we both graduate from Seaville High next year were made on another warm night, in June, in the back of the same hearse.

"How do I know you're really over Lauralei?" Harriet had asked me in the middle of things.

"What would I be doing here if I wasn't over Lauralei Rabinowitz?" I answered.

"You would be trying to make out here," said Harriet.

"What kind of a person do you think I am?" I said.

"I'll know when you answer this question: Are you going to marry me?"

"I'm not going to marry Lauralei Rabinowitz," I said.

"Are you going to marry *me*?"

"When?"

"A year from now," said Harriet.

"Yes," I said, "a year from now, yes."

"Are you going to ask my mother if you can?"

"I thought it was the father you asked if you could."

"My father's in Akron," said Harriet. "He won't be home for another week. I want you to ask my mother if you can tonight."

"All right, I'll ask your mother tonight," I said. "*Tonight?*"

"Tonight," Harriet said, "because she thinks you're just using me to get over Lauralei Rabinowitz."

Both Harriet's parents were C.P.A.s, and when you spoke to either of them there was usually an adding machine going. Everyone in Seaville used the Hrens as their accountants. The only thing they seemed to do besides add up figures was add to the population. Harriet had five brothers and two sisters.

"Fine," Mrs. Hren said when I announced my intentions, a cigarette dangling from her mouth, smoke curling up past her face, "but Harriet has to"—clickety clack the adding machine went—"finish high school, you realize"—*clickety clack*—"that, don't you, Wallace?"

Which was how I became unofficially engaged.

Engagements, according to Harriet, are not official until the girl gets the ring.

Our subject of conversation for the rest of the summer was The Ring.

One hot afternoon in August, we were once again discussing The Ring. Harriet was stretched out on the wicker couch, in the Hrens' one-room beach house at the ocean. She was all in white. When anyone is stretched out all in white in my house, it means they've "crossed over," as my mother likes to put it. I am the sixteen-year-old, only son of the leading Seaville mortician. My father prefers the description Funeral Director.

"Ideally, I would like to have the ring by the time school starts," Harriet was saying.

"Ideally, I would like to inherit a million dollars by the time school starts," I said.

"How much do you have saved so far?" Harriet said.

"I have thirty dollars so far," I said. "Engagement rings are supposed to be passé."

"My mother had one and my mother wants me to have one," Harriet said.

"Why doesn't your mother buy you one then?" I said. "Your mother probably has more than thirty dollars saved."

"I can lend you a hundred dollars," Harriet said. "We'll talk about it during the commercial." We were both watching a soap called *Hometown*. All the kids were watching it that year. The reception was fuzzy because the

9

Hrens had an old black-and-white set in the beach house which was hooked up to a battered antenna atop the roof. Every time a strong gust of wind blew in from the ocean, the actors shook and faded.

I was lying on the rope carpet with my feet up on an old streamer trunk the Hrens used as a coffee table. I was studying Harriet, trying to see her through the eyes of Lauralei Rabinowitz, who kept returning to my mind like mildew you can't get off a suitcase no matter how often you set it out in the sun and purge yourself of it. Maybe she was more a disease than simple mildew, a disease so far unrecorded in the annals of medical history. Years hence I would be told, "It's Rabinowitzitis, all right, you've been suffering from it since before your marriage. You have all the symptoms. I'm surprised you didn't notice a certain apathy alternating with periods of deep depression."

Harriet was prettier than Lauralei—Lauralei would have to give her that. She was petite and Lauralei was built like a phys-ed teacher; she was blond and hairless and Lauralei shaved every other day. She was blue-eyed and pug-nosed and Lauralei was brown-eyed and longing for a nose job. . . . But Harriet was a math lesson, and Lauralei was a whole course in chemistry, and it was Lauralei I wished I was trying to get out of buying a ring for.

"Harriet," said my mother, "is a nice girl and she'll be an asset in the business."

"That girl," said my mother some time back about Lauralei, "will never settle for Seaville. You think she'll come back to you after she goes to Ohio State?"

"Why do I have to think about those things now?" I used to say.

"Because now is when you're going to get in trouble if you don't get control over yourself. Stay out of the hearse, too, or I'll tell your father you've been in there with her."

Lauralei Rabinowitz did not come into my life until the middle of my junior year, when her family moved from New York City to Seaville. Before she first bumped up against me in the hall, laughing at me with her dark, sexy eyes and letting me have my first whiff of Arpege, the French perfume she touched to her ears every morning before she left the house, I was a simple son of an undertaker, the brunt of many jokes and used to it, a bookworm for compensation. My only accomplishment B.R. (Before Rabinowitz) was to win an essay contest in Mr. Sponzini's English class.

My composition was called "Evasions" and it was inspired by my mother's habit of refusing to say that anyone died. Someone "crossed over," "went to her reward," "passed on," "drew his final breath," on and on. I spent hours in the library elaborating on my theme, working myself into a sweat over the discovery that the Malays have no name for tiger, lest the sound of it might summon one; that in Madagascar the word "lightning" is never mentioned for fear it might strike; that Russian peasants have no name for their enemy, the bear (they call him "honey eater"); and that in Hungary the mothers of new babies were once told "What an ugly child," to placate evil spirits and make them less jealous.

"Brilliant work, Wally!" Mr. Sponzini wrote across the top of my essay, but it did nothing to stop Duffo Buttman from following me home singing to the tune of "Home on the Range" "Oh give me a home, where the corpses all roam, and the ghosts in the caskets do play . . ." and it did nothing to prevent Miles Wills from calling across a classroom, "What are you going to undertake today, Witherspoon?"

Before Rabinowitz, I consoled myself with the idea that one day every one of them would be wheeled Mr. Trumble's way. He was my father's assistant, in charge of receiving. But that was not a lot of consolation, considering the fact that Mr. Trumble was in his late sixties, and I was in line for Mr. Trumble's job, and even if Duffo Buttman himself were to arrive stiff and white and ready for the grave, I would rather die myelf than be a party to the necessary embalming.

"You'll get over it," my father would tell me.

"Oh no I won't," I'd say emphatically, "ever!"

"Wallace!" my mother said then, raised eyebrow, eyes narrowing to caution me not to get my father excited, his heart was weak.

Then Lauralei Rabinowitz came and did battle with my badly battered ego, suggesting the back of the hearse herself one night, and we fell in love the way a storm rages, or a rock number builds, the way you fly in dreams all by yourself, or go down a roller coaster smiling while you're screaming, with the wind trying to push you back and the earth turning before your eyes.

"Where is love?" I argued with her our last night in the hearse. "Where is love in all this talk of height and religion and profession?"

"Listen, Wally," she said, "Maury Posner's coming by my house in an hour to borrow my notes from Earth Science, so I can't continue this discussion." She was still combing her hair.

"Maury Posner's shorter than I am!" I yelled.

"He's Jewish, though," she said, "and he's already got a bid for the Zebe House at Ohio State."

"It's over," Harriet said. For a second I thought she was reading my mind (only my mind always shouted it: RABINOWITZ IS OVER!), but she was talking about the soap. It was all over except for a last tease, a brief look at the next day's episode.

On the screen was Sabra St. Amour. She played a teenager on the soap, this tall, green-eyed girl with very light blond hair spilling down to her waist. The same way The Fonz was always saying "H-eee-EEY" on *Happy Days* or J.J. said "Dy-no-mite!" on *Good Times*, Sabra St. Amour's trademark was "Tell me more." She'd milk those three words for all they were worth, and around school you'd hear kids saying "Tell me more" the same way she said it. There were "Tell me more" T-shirts with her face on them. There was a song called "Tell Me More," recorded by The Heavy Number. She'd done a T.V. special last winter called "Tell Me More," which was a series of really bad comedy skits, but it didn't matter because all she had to say was "Tell me more," and everybody would fall apart.

During the tease, Sabra St. Amour was hanging up a poster in her bedroom. She'd just moved to another town to start over, after her movie-star mother had shot another woman's husband in their love nest. The poster was an ocean scene, not unlike the one Harriet and I could see from the Hrens' beach-house window. There was surf washing up on the beach. Sabra was reading something printed on the poster while the crawl of credits was passing across her face.

"Accept me as I am," said Sabra in a slow, wistful voice, "so I may learn what I can become."

Then the music began to swell, and the theme of *Hometown* sounded on the organ, while the camera did a slow fade-out.

"I can lend you a hundred dollars toward the ring," Harriet said, punching the Off button on the remote control.

"Nobody else in the senior class is going to have a ring, Harriet," I said.

"My mother had hers by her senior year," she said. "She had a half-a-carat Keepsake."

"Why don't we take a walk on the beach?" I said.

"You wouldn't have to pay back the hundred till after we were married."

"It's a beautiful day," I said.

"I don't want to miss *Star Trek*," Harriet said. "Mr. Spock is going to desert the Enterprise for a strange, female creature from an alien colony."

"Do you mind if I take a walk?" I said.

"Alone?" Harriet said.

"Alone," I said, but it didn't turn out that way, even though Harriet stayed behind.

2. Sabra St. Amour

I never like to watch our show on tape, but Mama had gone through all the trouble of getting a television set for our beach house, and hooking it into cable so CBS would come in.

There I was in all my gory glory on a hot August afternoon playing a character who had only one thing in common with me: the name. Mama actually changed our name to St. Amour about a year after I landed the role on *Hometown*.

Back in The Dark Ages (just after my father was killed in a plane crash) I was fat little Maggie Duggy from Nyack, New York, complete with pimples and an inferiority complex. (It didn't help matters that Mama remarried eight months later.) Now I'm Sabra and Mama is Madam St. Amour, and we live in the famous Dakota apartment building on Central Park West in New York City.

For the month of August we were vacationing in Seaville, in the Hamptons, a two-and-a-half-hour drive from Manhattan. Mama likes to make the trip in my new little white Mercedes, with the top down, a tape of Frank Sinatra singing "My Way" playing, and Mama passing every car on the road, calling out, "Okay, you other mothers, clear the way! We're coming through!"

Mama enjoys success.

I was watching the ocean through our picture window, wishing I could smoke, pretending I was interested in my performance. Since I wasn't going to be doing the soap much longer, I wasn't that fascinated, but I didn't like to hurt Mama's feelings. She was sitting in the Eames chair with her feet up, taking notes while she watched, the way she always did.

Mama looks a lot like the actress Shelley Winters. Back in The Dark Ages when my stepfather, Sam, Sam, Superman was alive, he used to tell her she was another Marilyn Monroe. (That didn't stop him from plucking her out of the limelight into the two-bedroom Cape on a wooded half acre, complete with washer/dryer/dishwasher/self-cleaning oven and automatic garbage disposal.) Mama's plumper now, very blond with light blue eyes and a whole mouthful of perfectly capped teeth. She has a very kind face, the sort that makes it hard to turn her down, and she's always surprising me with something. That morning when I walked out onto our deck for breakfast, there was this large, gold cuff bracelet resting on top of my napkin.

"What's this for?" I asked her.

"It's for you, sweetheart. Do I have to have a reason to give my own kid a present?"

"It's beautiful!" I said. "Mama, it must have cost a fortune!"

"Read the inscription inside," she said.

It was engraved in very tiny letters:

For All I Know You're Rome
And Paris, Too, I'm Home
With Dreams and You—That's All I Need;
You Cut Yourself, I Bleed.

"Oh, Mama!" I said. "That's sad."

"The hell it is," she answered. "That's motherhood." She laughed, reached for a pack of More cigarettes, changed her mind because of me and the fact I'm not supposed to smoke anymore.

"You can have one," I told her. "There's nothing wrong with *your* health."

"I'm going to give them up, too, baby," she said, "and until I do, I'm not going to smoke in front of you."

I said, "I wish you would," but I knew she wouldn't. For five years, ever since I got my first part in a Broadway show at age thirteen, Mama has lived for me. That isn't as awful as it sounds, because before she lived for me, she was living for Sam, Sam, Superman, who was lucky if he could afford to take her out once a month for the $2.40 special at Howard Johnson's.

Near the end of the show, just when the crawl was starting with the credits, there was a shot of me and the poster Mama had bought me once for my dressing-room wall. The producer of *Hometown*, Fedora Foxe, had seen the poster during a visit to me, and immediately had a writer put it into the show. Fedora was always having things written into the scripts that the cast did or said; she liked to say no fiction in the world could match the drama of real life.

"Accept me as I am," I was saying on the television screen, "so I may learn what I can become."

"There should have been a long pause there," said Mama.

The theme music swelled up and there was a fadeout on my face with this superthoughtful expression.

"Did you hear what I said, honey?" Mama said.

"You said there should have been a long pause there."

"Do you know what I mean?"

"Sort of."

"I mean between 'Accept me as I am,' and 'so I may learn what I can become.' Right after 'am,' you should have looked up wistfully, beat, beat, another beat, and then, as though you were getting it all together in your head, into 'so I may learn what I can become.' See what I mean, sweetheart?"

"I see."

"Three beats, and then finish."

"Okay," I said, "I see."

"It was peachy the way it was—don't get me wrong, but it could have been just a little better."

I sighed, unintentionally, and Mama looked across at me with this concerned expression. "Why the sigh?"

"Oh Mama, it just seems silly now to worry about it."

"Who's worried about it? I said it was peachy."

"I know you did."

"I'm just your silly mother, The Perfectionist, don't pay any attention to me."

"Mama," I said, "have you told Fedora what Dr. Baird said?"

"I wrote her a long letter, honey. I don't want you to worry about anything. From now on we concentrate on getting you better."

"*If* that's possible," I said. "Sam, Sam, Superman's ulcers never did get better."

"You know, sweetheart," Mama said, "I wish you wouldn't call your stepfather that."

"You called him that."

"But that was different," Mama said. "I meant it affectionately."

"You must have felt a lot of affection for him while you were loading up the dishwasher every morning, knowing you could have been in front of a camera instead."

"It was my own idea to give up my career," Mama said. "Sam never asked me to give up my career. Your stepfather was a wonderful man, honey."

"Except he gambled away every cent we ever had," I said. "May he rest in peace."

"He didn't always have good judgment," said Mama, "but Sam would give you the shirt off his back."

"To iron for him," I said.

"Oh, honey, don't be bitter," said Mama. "We came out okay. Look at us!" Mama said, waving her hands around the room. "This isn't exactly chopped liver, baby!"

I saw her starting to reach for her pack of Mores again, then stopping herself. She'd gone half an hour already without a cigarette. I'd gone a week, with a few sneak smokes when I was out of her sight, which wasn't often. Mama and I did everything together, went everywhere together. When we were separated, we were on the phone together. It was as much my doing as hers—I have to be honest about that. I felt right with Mama close, unsure of myself when she wasn't around.

Mama said, "Maggie, sweetheart"—she always called

me Maggie when she was being her most sincere self—
"this is your vacation. Stop worrying. Ulcers heal. There'll
be other roles, better ones. You just toast yourself in the sun,
run on the beach and forget your troubles."

I stood up and turned off the set. I was going to take a
walk on the beach so we could both sneak a smoke. "Mama,"
I said, "won't you miss doing the show?"

"You did the show, Tootsie Roll, I didn't."

"You know what I mean, though. We'll be civilians." It
was an old term Fedora still used for anyone who wasn't in
the business.

Mama gave my rear end a swat with a copy of *Soap
Opera Digest*. "Don't you sneak a cigarette wherever you're
going now," she said. She knew me like a book.

"The last time I quit smoking, I went up to a hundred
and thirty," I said. "And remember the way I looked in
The Dark Ages? Sam, Sam, Superman used to call me The
Blimp."

"He didn't mean that in a bad way," Mama said. (I don't
know how anyone could mean it in a good way.) "I'm no
sylph myself. Once we've both kicked the filthy habit we'll
look like a pair of beached whales for a while."

We both started laughing then. We laughed for a long
time, longer than the joke was funny. I'm not sure what
Mama was laughing at, but I think I was laughing because
I was relieved. I got my ulcer around the time Fedora began
talking about extending *Hometown* a half hour. When Dr.
Baird told Mama he didn't advise my doubling my work
load, I expected Mama to go into a real tailspin. She didn't,
though; she just sat across from him saying, "I couldn't agree
more," but it never rang true to me somehow. Mama thrives

on show business. If she had to choose between going for a day without any food and reading *Variety*, she'd choose *Variety* . . . and Mama loves to eat, a lot!

I still remember the time Mama got a sort of crush on the leading man in *Hometown*. She was spending a lot of time on the set with him, going across to McGlades for drinks with him, talking for long hours on the telephone with him at night. His wife complained to Fedora about it, and Fedora told Mama she was going to end my storyline if Mama didn't do something about it.

Mama sent me to the set while she sat around The Dakota swallowing Valium and listening to old Tony Bennett tapes for hours on end, smoking and staring at the walls. We couldn't talk about it together. Mama could never admit that Nick was just this pompous creep who went around trying to make any female in his path fall in love with him. It gave me stomachaches to hear Mama defend Nick, and we went through a bad time when we hardly talked at all.

Then one day after months had gone by, Mama came to the set as though it had all never happened. She gave Nick a smile, that was it, and went back to being my mother, cleaning up my dressing room, fussing over my wardrobe, cueing me and brushing out my long, blond hair—the whole bit. She even called Fedora, who was on the coast at the time.

"Well," she said, "the news from this end is that the great storm has passed, the sea is calm, the little skiff is not capsized, sails are up. We're still very much in the race."

I don't know what Fedora's answer was, but I do remember the next thing Mama said.

She said, "Now get her that new storyline you're always

promising, toss in five hundred extra clams a month, and we'll be back in business."

It was right after that when Fedora started the whole "Tell me more" bit which made me famous.

The only flaw Mama has is that she's overprotective. She'd keep me under glass if she could, until she was sure I was able to handle myself to her satisfaction, which would be sometime when I'm forty.

Around the time I got my ulcer, Fedora was trying out this new young writer named Lamont Orr. She wasn't sure whether she was going to keep him as part of her regular stable of writers or not. The cast called him Lamont Bore, because he couldn't stand to have one word of his dialogue changed, even when it didn't play well. Here was this twenty-four-year-old, apple-cheeked kid, who'd never written anything but a few weird off-off-Broadway shows and some daytime television, trying to throw his weight around with talent that had been in the profession for years and years.

Fedora let him hang around the set to get the feeling of the show, and she sent us off for Cokes together to see what kind of a rapport we'd have. When Mama would try to come with us, Fedora would dream up some reason to have a conference with her. Once she just said flatly, "I want them to get to know each other, Peg! They *have* to, you know, if Lamont does her scenes."

Mama was always saying things to me like "I guess the kid's getting to you, hmmmm? He's okay if you can get past all that Brut he splashes on himself."

"Mama," I'd say, "how can a man with a permanent wave get to me?"

"Well it's the fashion now," she'd say. "Someday he'll probably blink his baby blues at you and you'll be giving him his home permanents yourself."

We had Lamont to dinner one night, and when he walked through our front door, the first words out of his mouth were, "What a lovely *pied-à-terre*, Peg!" Peg, he called Mama, when Mama was old enough to be his mother. *Pied-à-terre*, when he was born and raised in Bolivar, Missouri.

"Oh am I in love!" I said to Mama when he left. "Be still my beating heart! Mama, he compared himself to Dostoevsky. He said, '. . . Both Dostoevsky and I believe character development is primary to plot development.' Did you *hear* it?"

Mama said, "If he ever . . . if he ever makes even the smallest kind of pass, I want to know about it."

"Oh the whole world will know about it," I said. "He'll cry out, I'll kick him so hard."

As I was collecting my bathing suit and towel for a walk to the beach, Mama said to me, "Let me ask *you* something now. How do *you* really feel about leaving the show?"

"I think I feel relieved," I said.

"You *think* you feel relieved?" she said. "What do you mean you *think* you feel relieved?"

"I think," I said, "beat, beat, another beat, I'm relieved."

"Get outta here!" Mama said. "And good luck with your mouth!"

3. Wallace Witherspoon, Jr.

Instead of underwear in the summer, I always wear a pair of trunks under my jeans so I can take a swim at one of Seaville's beaches if I feel like it. This drives my mother up the walls. My mother says it's no way for the son of a funeral director to behave. Funeral directors' children, according to my mother, must lead exemplary lives because of the very delicate nature of the profession. Our home is supposed to be the sort of home one wants to see their loved ones resting in "at the end of the long journey"—to use another of my mother's euphemisms for death.

If you want to know anything at all about the protocol of running a funeral home, don't ask my father, ask my mother. I think my mother's the world's foremost authority on the *dos* and *don'ts* of funeral-home life. *Do* keep all the shades in the front of the house at the exact same level. *Don't* sit around in any front rooms watching television with the drapes open at night. *Do* keep "the coach" (the polite word for the hearse) in the garage with the garage doors down, at all times. *Don't* just throw out old "floral tributes" in the trash, but stuff them into a Hefty Lawn and Leaf Bag so they are not recognizable as old flowers. On and on and on.

Every time I slip out of my trousers on the beach, I hear my mother's voice in my mind crying, "*Wal*-ly! Oh, *no!*"

That hot August afternoon after I left Harriet's, I left my pants and shirt and sneaks in a ball on the sand, and walked down to the water's edge. The tide was coming in, and Lunch Montgomery, this old blind-in-one-eye, black-and-white hound dog, was running around in the surf barking. That meant Monty Montgomery had to be around somewhere, a prospect I didn't welcome.

A few afternoons a week I worked for Monty in the store he and his wife owned, called Current Events. Monty sold newspapers and magazines, greeting cards, games and office supplies. He also sold T-shirts, standard ones already printed up, or the kind you could have anything you wanted printed on them. I was the printer, the poor slob who fitted the letters on the shirt and then stream pressed them into it. For this I got $2.60 an hour. The fair thing would have been for Monty and his wife to pay me about triple that, since I acted as their go-between. I don't think they even talked when I wasn't around. When I was there, Monty would say things to me like "Ask her why she orders twenty copies of *Town & Country* every month when we only sell three." Martha, his wife, would come back with something like "Ask him if he's heard that slave labor is against the law, or hasn't that rumor spread to the beach where he spends all his time?"

Monty would say, "Ask her if she imagines my idea of the perfect life is working twelve hours a day in some hick store selling Sugar Daddies to runny-nosed kids?"

Martha would say, "Ask him when he's ever worked twelve hours a day anywhere."

"Ask her," Monty would say, "if she thinks I got an education at Yale to stand here marking half the *TV Guides* New England and half Manhattan."

"Ask him," Martha would respond, "if he could have done better with his striking Yale education why he didn't."

They were your real all-American happily married couple, the kind you saw eating out in restaurants across the table from each other without saying anything but "Pass the salt," or "Where's the butter?" Silently We Eat Our Sizzling Sirloins, Hating Each Other's Guts Department.

Lunch was really Martha's mutt, but he followed Monty whenever Monty took off for the beach, which was a lot in the summer. Monty would swim out and Lunch would stand in the surf barking, as though he was a scolding stand-in for Martha.

Lunch's blind eye was a light blue color; the other eye was black.

"Did anyone ever tell you you were hilarious looking?" I asked him.

The dog ignored me. Sure enough, there was Monty out in the ocean, riding the waves on a surfboard.

The only other person around was this blond girl, sitting on a towel. Everyone else was in the area where the lifeguards were, about a half mile down the beach.

I was standing there wondering what the chances were of going in the water without having to strike up a conversation with Monty.

Monty's conversations begin something like this: "Hi there, Wither-Away, seen any good corpses lately?"

A variation: "Hi there, Withering Heights, I'm dying to see you."

Then he'd hold his sides laughing, give me a cuff to my ear, and start in on my relationship with Harriet.

"You going to marry her?" he'd ask. "Lots of luck, fellow. I married my high-school sweetheart and it's been downhill ever since."

I wasn't in a mood for Monty ever; that day, I really wasn't.

I walked down the beach away from him, past the girl on the towel.

Then I heard her calling me. "Hey! Hey, there! Hey!"

I turned around and she was standing, taller than I was, this long-legged, slender, pale girl with large green eyes and a tiny mouth. She wore a black bathing suit and a large gold cuff bracelet. She looked as though she'd been hospitalized all summer, or imprisoned—kept somewhere where the sun never shined.

"I came down here with cigarettes and no matches," she said, walking up to me. "I don't know how I could be so dumb."

"I don't, either," I said.

"Well do you have a match?"

"It isn't dumb to forget your matches," I said. "It's dumb to smoke." I stood there trying to figure out why there was something vaguely familiar about her, even her voice.

"Thanks an awful lot," she said. "I had the feeling I could count on you the minute I saw you." She was holding a package of gold Merits in her hand.

"Do you think you can count on the tobacco companies to look out for you?" I said.

"I don't need someone to look out for me," she said, "I need a match."

She started to walk back to her towel. I didn't want her to go. It wasn't that I needed another girl who towered over me in my life again, but I had this really flaky feeling that I'd spent time with her. Déjà vu or something. My father and mother had a song when they were courting called "Where or When." My mother liked to play it on the piano and sing along. It was about meeting someone and feeling you'd stood that way with them and talked before, and looked at each other the same way before. That was sort of the feeling I had with this girl.

I tried to stall her. "A long time ago," I said, "cigarettes had simple names: Kools, Camels, Lucky Strikes, Old Golds."

"They're still in existence," she said. "Where have you been?"

"Where have *you* been?" I said. "You're the whitest girl on the beach."

"I was in an insane asylum," she said.

"You'd have to be a little crazy to let the tobacco companies manipulate you," I said. "Why do you think they'd name a cigarette something like Merit? Merit's supposed to mean excellence, value, reward. What's so excellent, valuable and rewarding about having cancer?"

"I've heard of coming to the beach for some sun," she said, "for a swim, for a walk. I never heard of coming to the beach for a lecture."

"Think of the names of the new cigarettes," I said, realizing I'd stumbled on an idea that wasn't half bad. "Vantage—as in advantage; True; More; Now. The cigarette companies are using hard sell, because they're scared that the public will wise up to the fact they're selling poison."

Not bad at all, Witherspoon. I complimented myself. "Live for the moment because you won't live long. Get *More*. Be *True* to your filthy habit."

"Just say you don't *have* a match," she said.

At that moment, Lunch came skidding in between us, chasing a rubber duck that had been tossed in our direction. He was wet and she let out a scream, while Monty came jogging up to us with one of his sadistic grins. He had on a T-shirt with YALE written across it. He had his usual ingratiating opener.

"Hi there, Wither Up And Die. Cheating on Harriet?"

Then he took a look at the girl and did a double take.

Monty is not subtle in any way. He is this big palooka who lifts weights every morning and measures his chest size once a week. He is a wraparound baldie, who uses the last few strands of hair he has left to wrap around his already-denuded crown. When he does a double take, his whole body participates. His shoulders swing, his neck jerks, his hands shoot up to his hips with his elbows bent outward, his mouth drops open and his eyes bulge.

"Why, you're Sabra St. Amour," he croaked.

"That's right," I found myself agreeing aloud in stunned amazement. "That's who you are."

That's who she was, not nearly as beautiful as she came across on the big boob tube, but it was Sabra St. Amour, ail right: the soft long blond hair and sea-colored eyes, the husky voice (not so sensual sounding when you realized it was caused by clogged lungs), the small, slanted smile.

I said, "But I just saw you on the tube," and stood there like any star-struck jerk, incredulous, and staring at her.

"That was on tape," she said.

Monty stuck out one of the elephant paws he has for hands and said, "I'm Montgomery Montgomery. How do you do."

She winced in pain as he crushed her bones and pumped her arm up and down. "How do you do," she said.

I managed, "I'm Wally Witherspoon."

"Hey, Sabra St. Amour!" said Monty. "How about that?"

Lunch began to bark furiously, standing there like Martha complaining about the whole idea of Monty striking up a conversation with a star.

"Shut up, Lunch!" Monty commanded. Lunch barked all the harder.

"Well." Monty tried talking above the noise. "Tell me more!"

Sabra St. Amour made a face as though she always got that wherever she went, and Lunch persisted, only then he began to jump up on Monty. Monty would shove him back, and Lunch would charge with more gusto, until Lunch was actually snarling, and Monty was really giving it to him with his knee in Lunch's neck.

"Don't *hurt* him!" Sabra exclaimed when Lunch let out a yowl of pain.

"Dogs aren't supposed to be on the beach." I put in my two cents.

"What are you doing here then?" Monty asked me, but he finally had to give up and jog away so Lunch would follow and desist.

Monty called over his shoulder, "Better not let Harriet catch you, Wither-Away!"

"Who's Harriet?" Sabra St. Amour asked, when we could hear each other again.

"Just some fellow I know," I said.

She laughed.

"Does he smoke?" she said.

"Sure he does," I said. "Harriet's very suicidal."

"Is he around?" she said.

"He's around someplace."

"Would he have a match?" she said.

"Harriet's out of cigarettes, not matches," I said. "He smokes Merits. May I take him those?"

Then I did a crazy thing, maybe out of excitement over who she was, maybe out of self-consciousness at who I wasn't: I began to try and get the pack away from her. She held on to it hard, and we began this tug-of-war, laughing and pushing each other, stumbling around together on the beach until she finally wrenched herself free and ran toward her towel. She scooped it up, along with a beach bag, and headed toward the hardpacked sand near the surf, running fast, but calling over her shoulder, "Good-bye!"

"Wait a minute!"

"I can't. Good-bye!"

I didn't follow her. I read somewhere in one of my mother's movie magazines that a lot of famous female stars sit home alone at night because ordinary guys are afraid to pursue them, afraid to be rejected or just figuring someone like that has a whole life going for her, and certainly doesn't need some average clown butting in.

That was my feeling as I watched her speed down the beach on her long legs; she was a fast runner, too. I had the feeling she didn't expect me to follow her, and wouldn't welcome it.

So I just stood there, going over the little interlude

detail by detail in my head, fixing the memory of her so I could tell someone about it: Harriet or my sister—my mother, most of all. My mother'd love it that I met Sabra St. Amour on the beach. She'd tell her hairdresser about it and they'd cluck and twitter over it for a whole wash and set.

Then I looked down and saw the large, gold cuff bracelet in the sand. It must have fallen off during our little wrestling match.

I picked it up and read the inscription inside.

4. Sabra St. Amour

After I left him standing on the beach, I walked back through the surf remembering this book an actor brought onto the set once. It was called *All About Sex After Fifty*. When you looked inside there was nothing but blank pages. I could write a book just like that called *What I Know About Boys*.

There was a time when we were all living in suburbia that I wrote a long love letter every day to Elvis Presley. I had his pictures plastered all over my walls, and I played his records so often even Mama complained. I went from Elvis to David Cassidy, and from David to John Davidson. After I started in daytime, I got a crush on an actor who played my father, and when his story-line ended, I lost so much weight Mama had to force cans of Metrecal down me on the set. . . . But none of it was ever real.

"You think it's real," Mama would tell me when I was down and dragging myself around, "but it's like the difference between plastic and wood, honey. The real thing is wood. When it happens to you, you'll know, because it'll splinter, crack and burn. You just be patient."

It's a pretty ironic situation, when you consider that my new legal name means Saint of Love. The only date I've ever been on was one with another daytime actor arranged by *Hometown's* publicity woman, for a *Soap Opera*

Digest awards banquet. We never saw each other before or after the affair, though there were various items about our "romance" in the gossip columns. Most of what you read in gossip columns is sent in by a press agent, and a lot of it is just made up.

When I got back to our beach house, Mama was waiting for me out on the deck.

"I thought you were just going for a *little* walk?" Mama said.

"I was. I did."

Mama looked at her watch, the face of which simulates the dashboard of the Porsche automobile, black with red hands and luminous white dots. The watch cost $325, which is cheap compared to some of Mama's watches. Mama has a thing about watches and shoes: She buys them by the carload. She has shoes she's never even worn, never even taken out of their boxes. When Mama was little she was the youngest of four girls, and she always wore shoes that had already been worn by one of her sisters. That explains her obsession with shoes. The watches are something else again. Maybe she had a compulsion to buy all of them because she looks at a watch constantly, trying to fit everything into our elaborate schedule: my classes at Manhattan School of Performing Arts; my acting lessons with Mrs. Chaykoffsky; my twice-a-week sessions with my shrink; my hair appointments and my fittings.

"Well you don't have to worry about getting a sunburn anymore," Mama said. When you do a soap, you have to worry about things like that. You can't have a sunburn unless your storyline has you in a resort area, or it's mentioned you were at the beach.

Mama wasn't the type you told about meeting a boy at the beach. I think anybody's mother would like the looks of Wally Witherspoon. A casting department would file him in the "All-American Boy-Next-Door" category, with his short, straight black hair; round, light blue eyes; longish thin nose and great wide white smile. But all Mama would think about if I told her we'd met was what was I doing striking up a conversation with a stranger! Hadn't I ever heard of rape and murder?

Mama was the type who'd read every word in the *Daily News* about some young psycho, look up from her paper at me and say, "Here's another one. All the neighbors say he was an angel, never missed Sunday school and adored his old mother, but he picked up a hatchet and committed bloody murder on an innocent girl he'd done God knows what to beforehand!"

My shrink warned me I was too dependent on Mama, but I wouldn't be anything, including able to afford a shrink, if Mama didn't watch out for me. Maybe I wouldn't need a shrink if Mama let up, but I probably wouldn't be an actress, either. Practically everyone on the show has a shrink, or was in analysis at one time or another. Mama says acting is a demanding profession, and it's good to get out all the kinks so they don't interfere with the discipline all actors need.

I don't think I really miss a social life—I don't know because I've never had one. But I would miss acting. I'll miss being on *Hometown*, too, I can't deny that. Once my ulcer quiets down, I'll try for something besides daytime T.V. I'd like to try Broadway again, or act in a film.

Mama likes to tell me to hold myself dear while I'm young.

"They don't make chastity belts anymore, Mama," I tease her.

"I'm not talking just about that," says Mama. "I'm talking about having a value on yourself, your whole self, not just what's below your waist. *You*. Sabra St. Amour."

"I don't even know who I am," I say.

Mama says, "You're a first-class talent. Someday you'll be a wife, and a mother, but before that day comes you'll build yourself a good, big bank account so you'll never have to depend on anyone for your security."

After I changed out of my bathing suit, I put on a robe and got out the backgammon set. Mama and I have always relaxed together by playing games: Careers, Scrabble, Monopoly, Yahtzee—you name it. That summer it was backgammon. We played for a few hours every night before dinner.

"Not tonight," Mama told me as I walked out onto the glassed-in sun porch overlooking the ocean. "Sit down, honey, and turn the tape down."

Ethel Merman was singing *Gypsy,* which was a play about a stage mother. You'd think Mama would hate it, because it wasn't a flattering picture of a stage mother. Rose, the main character, was a hard, driving woman who didn't care if her kids were happy, so long as they were stars.

Mama happened to love the story, though sometimes she'd laugh and say, "How'd you like it if I was like her?"

When I wanted to get a rise out of her I'd say something like "Oh, is there any difference, Rose?" and she'd give me her famous raised eyebrow, or the finger which meant "up yours," or a mock punch to my $5,000 all-caps mouth.

Mama doesn't happen to be at all like Rose, but if I want to bug her I call her that.

I turned down Ethel and sat on the footstool of the chaise Mama was stretched out on.

Mama said, "I have a Reluctant Admission."

"Ohmigawd, I thought we left Lamont behind us," I said.

One of Lamont Orr's off-off-off-Broadway flops was a musical called *The Wind of Reluctant Admissions*. He was hoping it would be another smash like the old hit *The Fantasticks*, but the critics hated it. One reviewer printed just one comment: "Zzzzzzzzzzzz." It was a stupid play about a mythical kingdom which would be periodically hit by a strong wind. Whenever the wind blew, the people made reluctant admissions about things they feared, or hated, or wanted, or couldn't help.

"Reluctant Admission," Mama persisted.

"What is it?" I said.

"We're going out for dinner tonight."

I didn't fall off the footstool or anything because we went out for dinner about three nights a week. I just waited for Mama to continue. Beside her, on the table, there was a More still smoking, though she'd tried to put it out when I entered the room.

"Mama," I said, "did it ever strike you that cigarettes have strange names lately? More and Now and Merit, as if we all need more cancer now, as if we merit it?" I didn't put it as well as Wally Witherspoon had, but it didn't matter, anyway, because Mama wasn't really listening.

"We're going to have a long talk about cigarettes soon," said Mama. "We might even enroll in Smoke-enders. But right this minute I have some news for you. Fedora Foxe came all the way out here by seaplane just to see you. We better be on our guard."

"She's delivering my obituary in person, probably," I said. I was trying to be funny about it, because neither Mama nor I were completely honest with each other when it came to our feelings about leaving *Hometown*. It wasn't just the money, though Mama would have to resist any impulses to buy $325 watches for a while. It was the hole it would leave in our lives, and the forcing of certain decisions like should I go to college? would Mama keep our large apartment in The Dakota if I did? what would happen to our lives now with no more of the familiar running around to keep appointments and stay on schedule?

"There's something in the wind when Fedora hops on a plane, Tootsie Roll," Mama said. "Fedora hates flying."

"Why are you so in awe of Fedora?" I said. I used to be. I remember when my knees would shake and my lower lip tremble around Fedora. After I became featured and "Tell me more" caught on, I began to realize Fedora needed me as much as I needed her. Mama said I should get that idea right out of my head, I could be replaced overnight, but Mama was talking from her experience. She'd married Sam, Sam, Superman in a weak moment when her role had been written right out of a Broadway show. It wasn't that big a role, but I don't think Mama ever recovered from the blow. Mama never felt really secure in her whole life; she still didn't.

"I'm not in awe of her," Mama said. "I'm terrified of her. She's a manipulator."

"How can she possibly manipulate us, Mama?"

"She can connive," Mama said. "We have to be firm."

"She's just an old lady, Mama."

"Some old lady!" Mama said. Mama fanned herself with a copy of *Daytime TV*. The air conditioning was on; it was actually on the frigid side on the sun porch, but Mama liked to fan herself in mock irritation the way grand ladies do in old Oscar Wilde plays.

"Okay, Miss Know-It-All," Mama said, "don't let anything faze you. But would you mind washing the sand out of your hair and getting into something elegant? We've got a seven-thirty date, and *I'm* impressed enough to want to be on time."

"I'll put on knee pads," I said.

"Meaning what?" Mama said.

"Meaning shouldn't we make our entrance on our knees with our eyes down?"

"What did I do to displease you, God?" Mama said, looking up at the ceiling. "Was it so bad I had to be saddled with this wiseacre kid?"

As I was going upstairs, Mama called after me, "Wear your nice new bracelet, honey. I want Fedora to see it."

5. Wallace Witherspoon, Jr.

I never liked bringing home kids from school because of the way they got quiet once they were in the house. I always had the feeling they couldn't wait to talk about it once they got out of there. ("They've got three rooms in front for the corpses!" et cetera.) But Charlie Gilhooley was the exception. He was another bookworm, another receiver of A pluses from Mr. Sponzini, and almost as big an authority on Seaville and its history as old Mr. Sigh, who lived with his sister and wore knicker suits year round.

"Ramps instead of stairs!" Charlie exclaimed the first time I ever dragged him home from the library with me. "Of course! To wheel the bodies around! Makes perfect sense!" Charlie was slightly on the enthusiastic side about nearly everything—that was his way—but it was better than just clamming up and pretending my house wasn't any different from anybody else's.

Charlie wanted to know everything there was to know. He wanted to know more than I wanted to know about the Witherspoon Funeral Home, and I'd have to tell him I didn't know the answers to half his questions because I had this deal with my father: I didn't have to take an active interest in the business until I was out of high school. Charlie'd ask, "How can you not want to know?" "I'll never want to know," I'd tell him, "even after I know."

Charlie was sixteen when he started telling a select group of friends and family that he believed he preferred boys to girls. The news shouldn't have come as a surprise to anyone who knew Charlie even slightly. But honesty has its own rewards: ostracism and disgrace. Even Easy Ethel Lingerman, whom Charlie dated because he loved to dance with her—Easy Ethel always knew all the latest dances— even Easy Ethel was ordered by her grandmother to stop having anything to do with Charlie.

My own deal with Charlie was don't you unload your emotional problems on me, and I won't unload mine on you. We shook hands on the pact and never paid any attention to it. I went through a lot of Charlie's crushes with him, on everyone from Bulldog Shorr, captain of our school football team, to Legs Youngerhouse, a tennis coach over at the Hadefield Club. Charlie, in turn, had to hear and hear and hear about Lauralei Rabinowitz. ("How can you be so turned on to someone with a *name* like that!" Charlie would complain.)

The same week Charlie made his brave or compulsive confession, depending on how you look at running around a small town a declared freak, Mrs. Gilhooley visited Father Leogrande at Holy Family Church and tried to arrange for an exorcist to go to work on Charlie. Charlie's father, a round-the-clock, large-bellied beer drinker, who drove an oil truck for a living and in his spare time killed every animal he could get a license to shoot, trap or hook in the throat, practiced his own form of spirit routing on Charlie by breaking his nose. It was a a blessing in disguise, Charlie needed at least one feature that was just slighty off, to look believable. The nose gave him that credibility, but people still always looked twice at Charlie, even before he spoke or walked. To use my sister's favorite, and maybe only, conversational adjective, Charlie's good looks are unreal.

Mrs. Gilhooley's idea of dinner is a paper plate swimming in SpaghettiOs, with a Del Monte peach half in heavy syrup thrown in for variety. The Gilhooleys live in a ranch house on half an acre up in Inscape, near the bay, and Mr. Gilhooley has crammed the yard with old cars, front seats of old cars, assorted old tires, a boat which no longer floats, rusted lawn mowers and broken garden tools, and an American flag, on a pole with the paint peeling off it, which has been raised one time only and never lowered. It flies on sunny days, in hurricanes and through the Christmas snows, a tattered red-white-and-blue thing that must resemble the rag Francis Scott Key spotted after the bombardment of Fort McHenry.

I won't describe the inside of the Gilhooley house. It's enough to say that it was one of life's little miracles that Charlie came out of that pit every day looking more like someone leaving one of the dorms of the Groton School for boys than someone leaving something that long ago should have been condemned by the Sanity and Sanitation Committee.

I think Charlie regrets having emerged from his closet, even though long before he did he was called all the same names, anyway. Charlie told me once: "You can make straight A's and A+ 's for ten years of school, and on one afternoon, in a weak moment, confess you think you're gay. What do you think you'll be remembered as thereafter? Not the straight-A student."

My father has an assortment of names for Charlie: limp wrist; weak sister; flying saucer; fruitstand; thweetheart; fairy tale; cupcake, on and on. He never calls Charlie those names to his face, naturally; to Charlie's face, my father is always supercourteous and almost convivial. After all, everybody's going to die someday, including the Gilhooleys; why make their only son uncomfortable and throw business to Annan Funeral Home?

Whenever my mother told me we were having corned beef and cabbage for dinner, I usually asked Charlie over that night. It was his very favorite meal. He crooned and swooned over the anticipation of it every time, just as he was doing that night in my bedroom.

"Oh, and the way your mother does the cabbage," he was saying, "not overdone, just crisp and with some green still in it, butter melting off it—" et cetera. Charlie can do a whole number on a quarter of a head of cabbage.

I was sitting there fondling the gold cuff bracelet, trying to figure out what to do with it, since there was no summer phone listing, no listing at all for Sabra St. Amour. She probably had an unlisted number; a lot of the summer people from New York City did.

I was also watching Charlie and wishing I was his height (6'3½") and had his deep blue eyes and thick golden hair. The Lord gives and the Lord takes. I wouldn't like Charlie's high-pitched, sibilant voice, nor his strange, small-stepped, loping walk. When you first see Charlie walk, you think he's into an impersonation of someone, or doing a bit of some kind, but he's not. The walk is for real.

Charlie says ever since the movies and television have been showing great, big, tough gays, to get away from the stereotype effeminates, he's been worse off than ever before. "Now I'm supposed to live up to some kind of big butch standard, where I can Indian-wrestle anyone in the bar to the floor, or produce sons, or lift five-hundred pound weights over my head without my legs breaking."

"'The media is trying to make it easier for your kind,'" I argued back.

"They're trying to make it easier for those of my kind who most resemble them," Charlie said.

My sister, A. E., came into my room just as Charlie was finishing his drooling over the cabbage with the butter melting on top. She said, "Forget it. The menu's changed."

Like my mother, A.E. (for Ann Elizabeth) has lots of freckles. My mother uses makeup against hers, but A.E.'s not allowed makeup because she's only ten. She tries lemon juice unsuccessfully, but mostly runs around covered with spots like a Dalmatian with very long orange hair and glasses because she's nearsighted. In the summer she looks like a little ghost someone painted red, which was how she looked that night, with her sunburn, in her long white, cotton caftan. She wears white frame glasses, too, insisting on them for some reason the rest of the family has never figured out. Since A.E. was a baby, screaming out one day that she did *not* want manilla! as we were about to give her a first taste of vanilla ice cream, she has been emphatic about her likes and dislikes, always strong and slightly mysterious.

She did not like corned beef and cabbage, either, so there was a victorious smile curling the corners of her small, pink mouth. "Due to the not unlikely, but nevertheless unexpected, arrival of a guest, we have had to change the menu." A.E. loved to talk like a book instead of like a ten-year-old, and she managed it for as long as she could sustain it at one time.

By "guest" she did not mean Charlie. . . . In our house, a "guest" meant only one thing. Someone had died, would soon be reposing in one of our Slumber Rooms, then off to the cemetery in our "coach." . . . When guests were with us, we did not fix anything for ourselves to eat which carried a heady aroma. We did not want to chance offending the bereaved. Replacing corned beef and cabbage that evening, A.E. informed us, was meat loaf, new potatoes and a salad.

"Who's our guest?" I asked.

"Old Mrs. Lingerman."

"Ethel's grandmother?" Charlie said.

A.E. nodded.

"Well hallelujah!" Charlie said. "Back to the dance floor."

"Why don't you just turn that gold bracelet in to the police?" A.E. asked me.

" 'Charles Gilhooley,' she used to say to me, 'your hair's too light to seem natural.' I'd tell her the truth, it was natural, and she'd say back, 'Well it's so light it don't seem natural, and if it wasn't natural then Ethel could not go out the front door with you even to cross the street, you realize that, don't you?' 'Oh yes, ma'am, Mrs. Lingerman,' I'd say, 'but my hair is my own color, ma'am.' "

"Sabra St. Amour might remember my name and call me," I said.

"Sure, sure," said A.E. "Sabra St. Amour might remember your name and call you and I might grow up to be Queen of England."

"I might, too," Charlie said.

"I'd just as soon she didn't call here, anyway," I said.

"Why?" Charlie said.

"Because then she might come here," A.E. said, "and there'll be Easy Ethel's grandmother, open coffin, too."

I groaned and sighed appropriately.

A.E. was delighted with my misery. "It's not a P.O., either," she added.

In mortician jargon, a P.O. is a Please Omit—meaning no flowers.

"This place will stink of lilies and roses and stock; it'll stink around here good!"

Even Charlie said, "Why don't you leave the bracelet someplace where she can pick it up? How about Current Events?"

"Wait until she finds out what you're helpless to prevent yourself from becoming when you grow up!" A.E. said, always making my father's profession sound even worse than it was, sound like vampirism which has to be passed on to each succeeding generation.

"There are female morticians, you know," I threatened A.E. for the umpteenth time.

"I've already made up my mind that I'm going to be an internationally renowned poet," A.E. said, "and besides it isn't woman's work."

"Where is women's liberation when I need it?" I said.

"You ought to be glad you've got something to look forward to being," said Charlie. "I'll end up like Mr. Sigh if I stay in this town."

"I'd rather be Mr. Sigh any day," I said. "*Any day!*"

"Mr. Sigh lives with his sister," A.E. said, "and I'll probably live in Paris, France." She swung through my door, letting in Gorilla, our enormous Persian cat. Gorilla walked across to my small round rag rug and swooned across it, stretching out full length with her tail whipping slightly at the tip.

I picked her up. "We have a guest coming, sweetheart," I said, in my best imitation of the old-movie actor Humphrey Bogart. "Try to stay out of the coffin; it repels certain people."

"Are you and Harriet going to The Surf Club Saturday night?" Charlie asked me.

"When don't we go to The Surf Club Saturday night?" I said.

"Maybe I could call Ethel and we could go double."

"Charlie," I said, "you said you were through dating girls."

"I can't take Legs Youngerhouse to The Surf Club," he said, "even if he'd go with me."

"What am I going to do with this bracelet?" I said.

"Go back to the beach tomorrow and look for her?" Charlie said.

"Yeah, maybe."

"So it's okay if I invite Ethel along for Saturday?"

"Do what you want to do," I said.

"I like to dance," Charlie said. "Shoot me."

My mother called upstairs, "Dinner, everyone."

"Charlie," I said, "I'm sorry about the meat loaf."

" 'Charlie Gilhooley,' Mrs. Lingerman used to say to me when I'd go over to pick up Ethel, 'Charlie Gilhooley, you walk as though you're trying to hold on to a fifty-cent piece with your bottom. I never knew anyone to take such teensy-weensie steps, leastwise not a member of the *male* sex.' "

We headed down the stairs to the dining room. "Well, Mrs. Lingerman, rest in peace," Charlie said.

I still hadn't decided what to do about Sabra St. Amour's bracelet.

6. Sabra St. Amour

Mama and I like hot foods like Indian curries and Mexican tamales, which was why she picked The Frog Pond for dinner that night—there wasn't anything spicier on the menu than rib roast. I was supposed to watch my diet very carefully.

The Frog Pond looks like an old-fashioned, gingerbread farmhouse, with a small lily pond behind it, and huge weeping willows on the bright green lawn around it.

You're not supposed to hear anything there but comforting, country sounds: the birds, the breeze ruffling the leaves, idle summer-night chatter, the chink of silver against china and ice cubes against crystal. Off in the kitchen was a whir of a blender beating butter and cream and salt into mashed potatoes . . . an oven door opening to pull out popovers . . . absolutely no music . . . and the waitresses whisper when they ask if everything is all right.

"Honey, show Fedora your bracelet!" Mama shouted across the table at me.

"You know, I've been giving this situation of yours a lot of thought," Fedora was saying at the same time.

They hadn't yet decided who would go first. I managed to slip in a lie. "I forgot to wear the bracelet, Mama."

"You forgot to wear it!" Mama said. "I reminded you,

sweetheart, don't you remember?"

"I didn't sleep very much this week, for thinking about everything," Fedora continued. She was a little woman with a very militant posture and a great deal of authority in this deep voice which seemed to come from someone behind her or above her.

We were sitting at a round table in the center of the dining room under the apprehensive eye of the proprietress. Both Mama and Fedora had second-balcony voices. Fedora was drinking her usual, a bright red Campari on the rocks, with a twist of lemon; Mama was having her Manhattan with the two cherries. I sometimes think Mama invented that just to be different, though she says she craves a taste of something sweet immediately before and immediately after whiskey.

I was toying with a ginger ale. Before I got my ulcer, I used to nurse a rum collins through other people's cocktails; on holidays, I'd have a glass of champagne.

Mama said to Fedora, "I gave her the most exquisite cuff bracelet, with a verse inside that's to die, and she forgets to wear it. Do you love it?"

"I finally came to a decision," Fedora said, ignoring Mama.

"About what?" Mama said.

"About what do you think? I've been trying to tell you that I've been going over this thing in my head. I've had some very sleepless nights."

"I'm sorry to hear that," Mama said, "but when exactly were you trying to tell me all this?"

"At the same time you were carrying on about some sort of bracelet."

"Some sort of five-hundred-and-fifty-dollar brace-let!" Mama said. "And I paid wholesale at that, and that's minus the expense of the engraving."

I always had the idea when we were out that everyone was staring at us, Mama always talked so loud, and always about money.

Fedora sighed.

Mama heard the sigh and sat forward like an obedient child. "Please continue, Fedora."

"I'll do the best I can," said Fedora, patting her short black hair to comfort herself, letting her fingers touch her own cheeks affectionately.

Fedora lived alone and liked to say in interviews that the cast of *Hometown* was her family. Fedora's face was very pale; she wore dark eyeliner and mascara, a touch of blue eye shadow and no lipstick. Mama said it was her style. I would tell Mama it was also most mimes' style, and Mama, who knew very little about anything to do with theater before the 1940's, would say Lord, Fedora had been around before mimes even thought of not talking.

Fedora was getting along, though nobody knew her true age. She had worked on radio soaps as a young girl, writing for some of the most famous.

She seldom wrote scripts anymore, but she rewrote them after finding the right writers, and she blocked out all the action.

"First of all," said Fedora, "Sabra, dear, how are you?"

"Doesn't she look well?" Mama asked.

"I'm fine, thank you," I said.

"No, no, no, no, no!" Fedora said. "I want to know really and truly how you are."

"I sent you Dr. Baird's report," Mama said. "It was all in there."

Fedora picked up my long, thin hand with her short, stubby one, the fingers of which sported great long, thick nails which curled over slightly like a parrot's claws, only they were painted luminescent white. She leaned across toward me and said in a hushed tone, "Now. How . . . *are* . . . *you?*"

"Fine," I said. "Just fine."

"She was on the beach for an hour today," Mama said. "She took a little hike all by herself for over an hour."

"You see, Sabra, I really *want* to know and really *must* know, what your thoughts are, your fears and hopes, and all there is to know about you." She paused. Mama was opening and shutting her purse, looking for a More, then deciding not to have one.

Fedora continued. "Did you hear me say that I not only want to know, I must know?"

Fedora was talking to me, but Mama answered, "Yeah, I heard that."

"Aren't you curious as to why I must know?"

"Is the Pope Catholic?" Mama said.

"Sabra?" Fedora said.

"Of course I'm curious," I said.

Fedora touched my sleeve. "I know news of this internal trouble has taught you not to get your hopes up, or your curiosity riled, or your wishes focused, because you are suddenly aware of your own fallibility." Fedora always sounded like the synopses of future episodes she often put together for the writers.

Mama said, "I wish you'd pee or get off the pot, because

the suspense is killing yours truly."

Fedora flinched slightly at Mama's vulgarity, then recovered and said, "Peg, in order to keep Sabra with us, we're going to forget about extending the show a half hour."

"*Really*?" I said.

"Now hold your horses," said Mama, "an hour, a half hour—she's still got an ulcer, and we made our decision."

"Peg, *Hometown* needs Sabra, and Sabra needs us."

"And I need to know my kid's healthy," Mama said.

"She'll get every attention, Peg. There will be a nurse on the set when Sabra's present, a full R.N."

"An ulcer isn't like that," said Mama. "I know because Sam had one, too. She just needs rest. She needs an easy schedule."

"Which she'll get," said Fedora. "From now on we'll cut back her appearances, and we'll depend a lot on just her voice, for telephone scenes and reveries. And listen to this—are you ready?"

"Shoot," Mama said, as though we were at the opening of a new war.

"I am going to add an entirely new dimension to Sabra's character. The way I intend to do it is the way my public would want it done: very honestly, no punches pulled, nothing held back: the truth. Sabra in *Hometown* will discover that she has a duodenal ulcer!"

"She will?" Mama said.

"She will," said Fedora, "and whatever happens to real-life Sabra will happen to Storybook Sabra. The stopping smoking, the gaining weight because of it, the—"

Mama interrupted her. "Fedora, Storybook Sabra never smoked."

"That will be taken care of. It will be discovered that she was a secret smoker for some time. We cannot settle for less than the full truth. I might have gotten away with a little blarney ten years ago—God knows twenty years ago it'd be three-fourths blarney—but I have to level with Mr. and Mrs. and Ms. America in this day and age." She reached out and gave my knee a squeeze. "Well, honey, what do you think?"

"You mean I'm supposed to gain weight on television?" I said.

"Be our guest," said Fedora.

"I don't want to gain weight on television, Fedora. I'd hate that a lot!"

"So we'll stuff you with a pillow, honey," Fedora said.

"I thought we were going to be perfectly honest."

"Oh, sweetheart, the public doesn't want that," said Mama. "I mean, the public is tuned in to you because their own lives are unbearable and realistic, how long do you think we'd last if we imitated their own lives right down to the letter?"

"I don't see how you can be honest and then stuff me with a pillow," I said.

"Don't be sidetracked by insignificant details," said Fedora. "This new Sabra is going to receive a lot of attention! There hasn't been anything like this on daytime since Melanie on *My Life to Live* had a facelift."

"We can't go one step further without asking Dr. Baird about it," said Mama, who hadn't even asked me. But I could feel the stirring of excitement starting somewhere in the vicinity of my ulcer, not an unpleasant feeling for a change, a certain uplift.

Fedora said, "I've already talked with Dr. Baird. He's agreed with me that if her schedule is cut down, and the tapings are done with minimal effort and no tension—a registered nurse will be on the set—and if Sabra wants to do it, then it's okay."

"He said you needed a registered nurse on the set?" said Mama.

"He didn't say that but we'll provide that. We're going to get a lot of mileage out of this, Peg, and it's positive: It instructs, and warns and helps viewers."

"Well I can tell you right now not to go to the expense of a nurse on the set. I mean what is the nurse for?"

Fedora gave another one of her long-suffering sighs. "We want any reporters or interviewers to know we're taking utmost care of Sabra."

"I get it," Mama said. "Publicity."

I was beginning to feel the way actors said certain agents made them feel: like a piece of meat, little more.

Fedora got my vibes and put her hand on my wrist. "Dr. Baird said *if* Sabra wants to do it, so I think Sabra has the floor now."

"Do you want to do it, honey? You don't have to. We've got plenty in the bank," Mama said.

Fedora said rather smugly, "I doubt that money is the motivating force behind Sabra's superb talent."

"We'll expect some additional clams, say five hundred extra clams a month," said Mama.

Mama put her hand on my wrist, and for a moment I looked as though I was being held down, one on either side pinning me to my seat.

"Maggie," Mama said, "I'm not talking you into this."

"No one is talking you into it," Fedora said.

"No one is talking me out of it, either," I said.

"You make up your own mind, Maggie," said Mama.

"Of course we'll help you by taking a lot of the burden off your shoulders. No rehearsals, no sitting around on the set for long hours," said Fedora.

"It was never my idea to quit in the first place," I said.

"No, but it was your idea to get an ulcer," Mama said, "and it's my responsibility to see that you ease up."

"Which she'll do," Fedora said emphatically. "Now. Oddly enough we already have the very best writer possible for this new storyline. I was going to get rid of him, but he handled the whole lobotomy segment for Wanda a year ago on *Other Worlds*."

Fedora was always announcing the names of daytime writers the way Walter Cronkite might mention a Nobel Prize winner, the major difference being no one really knew who Fedora was talking about.

I started to tune out and worry about calling Wally Witherspoon to see if he'd found my bracelet, when I heard Mama roar, "*Oh* no!"

"You know who I'm talking about," Fedora said.

"I most certainly do," said Mama.

"Who are you talking about?" I asked.

"Mr. Bore," Mama said.

"Lamont," Fedora said. "You always got along well with Lamont, didn't you, Sabra?"

I shrugged. "I can take him or leave him."

"Leave him," Mama said. "He gave you your ulcer."

"*La-mont*?" I said. "You've got to be kidding!"

"She started having stomach trouble when we talked

about extending the show," Fedora said.

"That was when *I* started having stomach trouble," Mama said. "She already had her ulcer."

"I don't know what gave me my ulcer," I said, which was the truth. If something besides your physical shape really does create an ulcer, I'll never know why I got mine. It showed up in the spring, after an ordinary winter. It wasn't so ordinary for Mama, I guess. It was the winter she decided to take some courses in the evening at The New School. "You're learning everything from how to count to a hundred in Latin to how to do a perfect pirouette," Mama complained one day, "and I'm a stopped clock. So I'm going in for a little self-improvement."

Mama went through some sort of middle-age crisis, I think. After she started classes she dyed her hair bright blond, fasted to lose weight, gave herself twice as many facials as usual, did exercises nightly—the whole bit. She went to the library nights when she didn't have classes to put herself in an atmosphere where she could study her lessons. I don't think it did Mama any good to be around all those young bodies and fast minds at The New School. She'd get out of patience with me when I'd tell her to drop out, the strain was showing. She'd blow up at me one day, then the next day buy me a present for blowing up at me.

It was the first time in our lives we didn't have dinner together every night. Maybe the ulcer came from all the frozen dinners I heated up. I used a tape recorder to cue me when Mama couldn't, and I still got all my lines perfectly for the next day's taping.

Mama called for more drinks and sat up straight, lighting a cigarette.

"There are any number of better writers who can handle this storyline, Fedora. Ellis Fountain did an hour special for CBS on this very subject!"

"Ellis has done no daytime, Peg."

"Lamont is only a kid!" said Mama.

"With a kid's vernacular," Fedora said. "He can do the medical scenes and Sabra's."

Mama's eyes were getting bigger and her voice was getting louder. When the waitress brought another Manhattan to her, Mama didn't even say please when she sent it back for the second cherry.

The whole thing got to me. I stood up and excused myself.

"Let me see inside your purse before you leave the table," Mama said. She told Fedora, "I don't want her off sneaking a smoke."

"If she goes off and sneaks smokes, we keep that in the script," Fedora said.

I showed Mama the inside of my purse. I might have had a pack of Merits in there, but something Wally Witherspoon had said on the beach that afternoon registered. I didn't feel like being a pawn of the tobacco companies.

"Good girl!" Mama said. "You go powder your nose now."

"Peg," said Fedora when she thought I was out of hearing distance, "Sabra's eighteen years old and you keep her like a twelve-year-old!"

"Oh really?" Mama said. "Then she keeps me like an octogenarian!"

7. Wallace Witherspoon, Jr.

When she called from The Frog Pond she said she didn't have long to talk. I said I didn't, either. My father was right behind me, working himself into a lather over the fact the flower car we usually rented for big funerals was in a repair shop. Floral tributes were pouring in for Mrs. Lingerman, including one made of white carnations and shaped like a harp. She'd belonged to every organization she could join within a fifty-mile radius, and it was as though all the old ladies in our part of Suffolk County had trotted off to their florists with twenty-five dollars.

I don't think Sabra St. Amour ever expected to see her bracelet again. She sounded surprised and delighted, so much so that she invited me to be her guest, go to a movie with her the next afternoon. She said it was the only time she had open. Since Seaville had just one movie, what she'd asked me to go to with her was *Oh the Stars and Stanley Two*.

This was when I blew my chance to be seen around the town with a superstar. (Eat your heart out, Lauralei Rabinowitz!) My father was standing at my elbow, glaring at me, with the Yellow Pages open to Funeral Directors. He'd been in the midst of calling around and asking colleagues how they were fixed for a flower car when her call came. *Oh the Stars and Stanley Two* was a science-fiction film with an R rating. Old Mrs. Pickens, the ticket taker at Seaville Cinema, knew us all and never let any of us under seventeen into an X-rated or restricted movie.

When I mentioned the fact it was an R, Sabra St. Amour's answer had been "I don't care if you don't." What I should have done was suggest something else to do, but by then my father's mood was rattling me, and I was humiliated to realize she was seventeen or older.

So I blew it. I said, "Why don't I just leave your bracelet with Monty Montgomery at Current Events on Main Street. You can pick it up first thing in the morning."

"Fine," she said, "and thanks again for taking care of it for me."

Click.

I stood there looking down at the phone's arm in disbelief that she could have come into and gone out of my life so fast.

"Give me that thing!" my father said, and yanked the telephone from my hand. . . . That was that. The next morning, early, my mother dropped off Sabra's bracelet at the store, on her way to the A&P.

"Withered brains, you are a real jackass," Monty greeted me when I went in to do my stint at the steampress machine the next afternoon. "You let something slip through your fingers you'll never get a chance at again."

"Ask him how come he hung around here all morning and didn't go to the beach," Martha said from behind a huge stack of Sunday *Times* parts she was busy assembling.

"Tell her I'm hungry for the sight of some female who

still cares about keeping her figure," Monty said.

"Tell him it's easy to keep your figure when you're able to stay home and not do man's work all day," said Martha.

"Oh ho ho!" Monty laughed. "Tell her that Sabra St. Amour happens to do man's work, or doesn't she know there are male actors?"

"Okay, enough," I said. "How many shirt orders are there?"

"Five," Martha said. "One's in French so be careful you get it right."

"She brought us a little present," Monty said. "We put it up over your work table."

There was a photograph of her stuck on the wall with a thumbtack.

She'd written across it: "To Martha and Monty and Wally, with thanks from your friend, Sabra St. Amour."

"Was she alone?" I asked Monty.

"All alone and lonely," he said.

"Ask him to tell you how he made a fool of himself fawning over her," Martha said.

"Tell her to shut her yap or I'll shut it for her," Monty said.

My first order was for an extra-large black cotton T-shirt with "Am I Glad I Married Pearl Cohen!" printed on it in white letters.

"Don't serve me any beans," Mrs. Hren said at dinner Saturday night. "They repeat on me."

Mr. Hren passed her a plate with nothing on it but tossed salad. "Why would you fix something for a main course that repeats on you?" he said.

"It doesn't repeat on anybody else," she said. "Look at me. I can miss a meal."

There was no arguing that. Harriet's mother was fat. Her once-fine features were now swollen beyond recognition.

When I was dating Lauralei, my father was fond of saying that you could tell what a girl would look like in twenty-five years if you saw her mother. (Mrs. Rabinowitz had blond streaks through her wiry black hair, wore long, thick false eyelashes, and favored red and orange dresses gussied up with fur capes made from the skins of tiny animals, their little dead feet and tails still attached. . . .) My father shut up on that score the moment I began dating Harriet. I don't think he was doing it out of consideration for Harriet or her mother. He was doing it because he would like me to marry Harriet and hang around Seaville the rest of my life doing you-know-what. He is not enthusiastic about college for fear I will completely lose interest in coming back, doing my twelve months in mortuary school, then returning to Seaville and starting work in the shop. That's what he calls the place behind our house where our guests are prepared for the Slumber Rooms. I go there as little as possible, then only to shove something at him through the door: his lunch, his mail, a sweater on cold days.

Besides Mr. and Mrs. Hren at the dining table that night were Harriet and me, Harriet's five brothers and her two sisters.

Once everyone had a plate in front of them, they shoveled the baked beans up with their forks as though pausing between mouthfuls had gone out of style.

Harriet had lately started wearing plastic rollers in

her hair in front of me. She sat opposite me with her hair wrapped around them, a crumb of B&M canned brown bread at the corner of her mouth, complaining because she had to be in the company of Easy Ethel Lingerman that night.

"What do you kids know about morals, anyway?" Mr. Hren said through his steaming glasses. He bent over so close to his plate to eat that the warm casserole steamed his horn-rimmed spectacles.

Even though there wasn't an adding machine in the room, I could always hear the *clickety-clicks* in between the Hrens' words. About the only time they didn't have their hands on the handle of an Addo-X was when they were eating or sleeping.

"Who cares about morals?" one of Harriet's brothers said. I could never remember their names, though all the Hren children's names began with H.

"Your sister just made an objection to being seen with Easy Ethel Lingerman," said Mr. Hren. "I say what difference does it make? Morals, schmorals, right? Isn't that what you kids think? Morals, schmorals."

"Don't provoke at dinner," Mrs. Hren said. "Provoke anytime else but not at dinner. You get everyone excited, we swallow air and get gas."

"Ohhhhh muth-*ther*," Harriet's little sister Hannah groaned.

"If there's a better, more proper way to put it, put it," Mrs. Hren said.

"When I was your age this kind of thing wouldn't be discussed in a family situation—ever," said Mr. Hren, "so count your blessings."

"Who wants to eat baked beans and discuss sex?" said Harry or Harold Hren.

"Were we discussing sex?" said Mrs. Hren. "Who said anything about sex?"

"Morals, sex—same difference," said Harvey or Hadley Hren. "I'd rather hear more about Wally's meeting with Sabra St. Amour."

"Tell me more!" Hedy Hren did an imitation of Sabra.

"I just met her, that's all," I said. I'd been sitting there washing down the beans with a glass of RC cola, remembering Harriet's saying once that she wanted ten children; five girls and five boys.

"Was she happy-looking or unhappy-looking?" Mrs. Hren asked me.

"Would you be happy-looking or unhappy-looking if you were making about twenty-five thousand a year?" Harriet said.

"That's peanuts in her field," said Mr. Hren. "She nets closer to forty, forty-five thousand."

I was imagining myself thirty years from now, sitting around the table with Wanda, Winifred, Wilbur, Warren, Wylie, Wendy, Wharton, et cetera, Harriet at the head of the table, entertaining Wendy's boyfriend or Wylie's girlfriend, speaking from my vast experience in the mortician business on some related subject, say the cost of seamless solid copper caskets, a summer's night, a day in the life of an average Seaville citizen.

"Was she stuck up?" Mrs. Hren asked me.

"No," I said.

"As a reporter about anything, stick to undertaking," said Hector or Harry Hren. He was Hector, probably, the only imaginative one of Harriet's brothers.

He wanted to be a cartoonist; he didn't want to see his sister marry into the funeral-home business. Harriet told me he'd come into her room at night, after his date, after he'd gotten a little loaded on tequila sunrises, and he'd try to reason with her about what life would be like with me.

Harriet was looking forward to it. She even wanted to take some beauty-school courses so she'd be a first-rate cosmetician. My mother was always saying she could teach her; it's real easy, anyway, my mother was always reassuring her. It's like doing up your own face, said my mother ... and I'd walk out of the room so I didn't have to hear about it.

Mr. Hren wanted Hector to apologize to me for being sarcastic.

"Skip it," I said.

"Apologize," said Mr. Hren.

"This isn't good for the digestion," Mrs. Hren said. "Hector, say you're sorry you're sarcastic sometimes."

"You're sorry you're sarcastic sometimes," said Hector.

Mr. Hren smirked. "You darn kid," he said, pleased. "You darn kid, you're some smart-A, aren't you?"

My own little future Wharton was telling me he wasn't going to follow in my footsteps for anything in the world, and I was telling him back: You don't have to. If you don't want to, there's Wylie, or Warren or Wilbur, or ... on and on.

"How's my grandmother doing?" Ethel Lingerman said while Charlie held open the car door for her. She was carrying an open can of Schlitz, and she flopped herself down on the front seat of Charlie's small red Fiat.

"Hi Harriet. Hi Wally. Well? How's she doing?"

"She's resting comfortably," I said. "She's gone to her great reward."

"Is a cat sleeping with her?" Ethel asked.

"No, the dog from next door is," I said.

"The rumor is cats sleep in your coffins with the dead people," Ethel said, taking a long swallow of beer.

"Pork Chop died last year and Corned Beef was run over by our ambulance this spring," I said. "So that just leaves Gorilla."

"I hope he's not in with my grandmother because she hates cats."

"It's not a he, it's a she," I said. "Your grandmother won't even notice."

"I think it's high time we stopped making these sorts of jokes," said Harriet. "These sorts of jokes are in very poor taste."

"Get her," Ethel said to Charlie. "It's my grandmother."

Ethel was a Clairol redhead in a pair of tight red slacks with some kind of pink halter above them which exposed her middle and pinned back her enormous melon-shaped breasts. She had two pairs of earrings on each ear, one which dangled down past her hair, one rhinestone stars that nestled against her lobes. She had on a lot of blusher, and gobs of gooey black mascara, plus eyeliner.

Harriet became suddenly vastly interested in the scenery as we rode toward The Surf Club, staring at it intently while she pulled at her fingers in her lap. Charlie started a long monologue on Dance Day, which was a tradition every year at the end of the summer in Seaville. The Kings and Queens of Dance were crowned the evening of Dance Day;

all day long there were dances of every kind performed on the village green. Charlie was trying to whip up some interest in the contest; Charlie was always trying to be someone in Seaville besides The Resident Fairy.

"I'd like to think of a superoriginal dance to perform," said Charlie.

"Boy, will my grandmother roll over in her grave when she knows I was out with you tonight," said Ethel. "Where'd you get the car?"

"I saved for it," Charlie said. He worked for Loude's Landscaping, digging holes and planting trees for six dollars an hour.

"I hear Lauralei Rabinowitz and Maury Posner are going to do the Charleston in that contest," said Ethel. "Do you ever see Lauralei around anymore, Wally?"

"That's all over with," said Harriet, grabbing my hand with the fingers she'd been pulling, to prove it.

"I wasn't asking you," said Ethel. "I was asking Wally."

Harriet stabbed my stomach with her elbow, holding my hand in a viselike grip. "That's all over with," I said.

"Oh my my my, we have a parrot along with us this evening," said Ethel. She thrust her can of Schlitz back under my nose. "Polly want a beer?"

"Polly would probably catch something grotesque from that beer can," said Harriet.

"Polly would probably catch something grotesque from that beer can," I said.

Ethel slapped her knee and laughed and held the beer can up to her mouth, swallowing chug-a-lug.

"Don't play into her hands that way," Harriet whispered to me. "What's the matter with you, anyway, Wally?"

"Every time I eat at your house I get confused," I said. "I feel like I'm going to suffocate or something."

"We won't eat with our kids," Harriet told me. "I don't like a big crowd around the table anyway."

8. Sabra St. Amour

"The in place with the locals is a place called The Surf Club," Lamont Orr said after we'd finished eating charcoaled steaks out on the deck. "How about popping in there for a while later?"

"Oh shush and listen to these words," Mama said. She had on a tape of Frank Sinatra old favorites. She shut her eyes and moved her face in heartfelt frowns while Sinatra sang "A Foggy Day in London Town." The new Elton John tape Lamont had brought us for a gift still had its cellophane wrapper on.

Lamont stuck his feet out and admired his Roots shoes. Then he put his right arm up on the arm of the director's chair and admired his wrist hair, and his gold Cartier signet ring.

Lamont was a walking/talking borrower of other people's glory. He always wore the little knit shirts with the Lacoste alligators on them, the Frye boots, the Gucci loafers, the Burberry sweaters, everything had someone's famous label or signature or symbol on it. When he spoke he often began sentences with "I think it was Camus who said," or "As R. D. Laing once said," or "Wasn't it Freud who said—" Lamont never seemed to wear anything or say anything original.

If you went out to dinner with Lamont in a restaurant where Lamont faced a mirror, you lost Lamont for the whole evening. He was always watching himself in the mirror.

He seemed to always shop until he found just the right shade blue to match his eyes, or rust to match his newly curled hair. He used QT so he was bronze all winter, and in the summer he was Mr. Wonderful on any beach with his tall, lean, brown body.

Something inside Lamont told him that he was hated by nearly everyone, so Lamont invented these psychological games and tests to help people forget they felt like barfing when he was around.

The first time he ever came on the set, he must have sensed Mama's overprotective nature right away. He completely ignored me and got her all involved in drawing a house. What kind of a house, Mama asked him and he said any kind she wanted to, and Mama got out this piece of paper and worked on this house through most of my rehearsal. Then Lamont studied it like he was some big-shot psychologist, interpreting one of those Rorschach inkblot tests. He frowned and *tsk-tsk*ed over it, and finally he said, "You are a very warm person, very warm, because look at all that marvelous chimney smoke. Some people draw chimneys with no smoke coming out and some people don't even put chimneys on their houses, but you are a person of extraordinary warmth. I can tell that instantly." Then he told her she was someone who liked people because she had sidewalks leading up to her house, and she made it easy for people to visit her because she had doorknobs on the doors, and she was an optimist because there was the sun drawn over the house. By the time he was finished telling her about herself, Mama was leaning so far over toward his director's chair, she looked as though she was about to spill into his lap. He reached out and pushed back a lock of her hair which had fallen forward, and it was as though someone had hit Mama over the head with a mallet. Mama straightened up and stared at him and thanked him for "administering the test" (Mama always got terribly formal when she was seething inside), and that was the last time Mama went anywhere near him, unless he was near me. Then she bird-dogged him.

It was Fedora's idea for Lamont to come out to Seaville and talk with Mama and me about the storyline. He was supposed to renew his acquaintance with us and get our ideas, and see if we could all work it out.

He was being diplomatic by not bringing up anything about the show his first night in town; he was pretending he'd been planning to come out that way all along, and delighted to know we were in the vicinity.

When the Sinatra tape was finished, Lamont tried again. "Everybody says the in place with the locals is The Surf Club." Lamont didn't even know anybody in Seaville besides Mama and me, but if he read about something in a newspaper or magazine, or heard just one remark, he always said "everybody says" or "they say" as though he had his fingers on the pulse of the world.

"Do you want to whip over there later for some action?" Lamont asked.

"How about a little action, keed?" Mama said to me.

"You go," I said.

"Not without you," Mama said.

"We don't have to make up our minds right away," Lamont said.

Mama got up and began clearing away the dirty dishes. "Please don't talk about me while I'm gone," she sang out.

"Why don't you leave the dishes?" Lamont said. "Just leave them in the sink?"

"Why don't I oink?" Mama said. "Why don't I run around on four legs with a curly tail?"

Lamont laughed and laughed at that and Mama carried out the plates.

Lamont studied his manicure for a moment, holding his fingers up in front of his eyes. Then he said, "If you had to spend the rest of your life in a prison or in a hospital, which one would you choose?"

"Why?" I said.

"It's a test," he said. "I gave it to your mother while you were dressing."

"I'd have to think about it," I said.

"Take your time," he said.

"Whose test is it, your test?"

"It's a famous psychiatric test," he said.

"What did you say?"

"You have to answer first."

"A hospital," I said.

"I said a prison," he said.

"What's a hospital mean?"

"People who say a hospital are usually passive types. They like to be waited on. They're choosy. Fussy. They like their comfort," Lamont said.

"What about people who choose a prison?"

"Ah!" Lamont said. "They're aggressive. They like discipline. They try to get along with most people. They feel guilty. They scheme."

"Are you giving her the test?" Mama yelled in from the kitchen.

"What did Mama say?" I said.

"She said a hospital, too," Lamont said.

"I said a hospital," Mama said. "What did you say, sweetheart?"

The thing about Lamont was you couldn't concentrate too long on how you wished he wasn't around. He always found a way to distract you.

The Surf Club was packed with people of all ages. It was right on the dunes about seven miles down from our beach house. Lamont and Mama and I were squeezed between some teenagers and a big cigar-smoking, red-faced man and his wife. The man was wearing a T-shirt which said "AM I GLAD I MARRIED PEARL COHEN!" They were drinking champagne to celebrate their twenty-second wedding anniversary. Lamont began a conversation with them right away.

Mama looked across the table at me and said, "Isn't this fun?" She had to shout to be heard.

When our drinks came, Lamont was reading the cigar smoker's palm and Mama paid the bill.

"Are you having a good time?" Mama asked me, cupping her hands to use them like a megaphone.

I smiled back at her, and we sat opposite each other for a while watching the dance floor.

About ten minutes later, Wally Witherspoon went dancing by with this short, black-haired girl.

I put my hand up to cover my profile, and sat there sipping my ginger ale. I felt funny about speaking to Wally. Mama didn't even know I'd met him. She didn't know I'd lost the bracelet or he'd found it. It really wasn't like me to keep secrets from Mama. I think the only reason I did was because I didn't want her to have a moment's worry about the bracelet, if I could help it. Then I just got into it, and it seemed easier not to mention it at all. Mama wouldn't have understood my offering to take someone she didn't even know to a movie.

The reason I asked him was because I knew Mama was driving Fedora down to Huntington that next day. I thought I could repay Wally that way for returning the bracelet to me. When he said he couldn't make it, I waited a few beats to see if he'd suggest another time or something besides the movie, but he didn't. I'd never asked a boy to go anywhere with me. I felt as though I'd made a tremendous goof. I felt like Mama, too, offering to pay for everything all the time. Mama was always saying to people, "Let's all go out for dinner—my treat!"

I felt like an old "lonely at the top" cliche, the super-star-whose-phone-never-rings sort of thing. I even had the idea he might have told his friends about it, that maybe they'd all had a good laugh over it.

While I watched him dance, out of the corner of my eye, I remembered the man who owned Current Events teasing him about someone named Harriet. I supposed that was Herself. She had this smug little air of self-possession about her, but she was ordinary: pretty, but not beautiful, what Mama'd call run-of-the-mill. I couldn't help wondering why he wouldn't even go to a movie with me, what there was about her that made him so loyal. For all I knew I was the victim of my own publicity, believing all the lies which weren't true: a dud posturing as more, the pits thinking she's the mountaintop.

Right at that point the band stopped playing, and the leader stepped up to the microphone. "Tell me more!" he shouted.

My stomach did a flip.

Mama gave me a little wink, and Lamont held up his palm and clapped one hand against it silently.

"That's right, ladies and gentlemen, we have a celebrity in our midst this evening, Miss Sabra St. Amour. Tell us more, honey. Stand up and tell us more!"

Mama and Lamont beamed and the man who was glad he'd married Pearl Cohen took the cigar out of his mouth, leaned forward and stared at me.

"Give 'em a thrill, baby!" Mama called across the table to me.

"Tell me more!" people began calling out.

"Come on up here to the bandstand and take a bow, Sabra!" said the bandleader.

After the first punch of fear, I felt the familiar cool flooding through me, and the little kick. I was on my feet, all smiles.

9. Wallace Witherspoon, Jr.

I guess there's a Deke Slade in every high-school graduating class. He's the jock and the bully and the one about fourth from the bottom scholastically. Deke was the son of the leading florist in Seaville, so I knew him pretty well. Our fathers did a lot of business together.

I suppose someday Deke and I will be working out the same little deals. I'll be asking relatives of the deceased if they want me to make the floral arrangements (discouraging the idea of a Please Omit funeral) , then getting Deke on the phone, throwing the business his way for a small cut. (Our slogan is "Death Is Just Another Tomorrow." Theirs is "Don't Wish Tomorrow You'd Sent Flowers Today.")

If it wasn't for this future collusion Deke and I had to look forward to, I'd have been a perfect target for Deke. At school, I'm not part of the gang that piles into cars to cruise around during lunch hour, nor one of the bunch that loafs around in the hall getting off hilarious one-liners that the others all crack up over. In that great High School Filing Cabinet where every one of us is typecast, I'm under G for gross.

I figure no matter what becomes of Charlie, years and years and years from now, there's one name he'll never forget: Deke Slade. Of all the "outies" Deke had to choose from, he chose Charlie to torture. Through four years at Seaville Senior High, Charlie was the mouse and Deke was the cat playing with the mouse.

Deke began making cracks the moment we arrived at The Surf Club. We were all drinking beer—Charlie had to go to the bar and get them for us, because he was the only one with a driver's license proving he was eighteen. When Charlie got up from the table, Deke would swagger over and make cracks about Charlie to Ethel. He'd ask Ethel things like who was the girl she came with and did they wear each other's clothes?

When Charlie'd come back carrying a tray of beer, Deke would call out, "Waitress, will you take my order, dear?"

Charlie and I tried to ignore Deke, the same way you try to ignore black clouds that suddenly appear out of nowhere on a sunny day at the beach, or a crazy who gets on the same bus with you and starts yelling that you killed God. Harriet had no love for Ethel, but her back was up because Deke was causing a scene, so she came back with a few remarks of her own. "Oh boy, Deke, are you insecure!" and "How come you don't have a date tonight, Deke?" It was like an assault on the Rock of Gibraltar with a feather duster. Deke just blinked at Harriet and got his mouth in gear for another series of insults aimed at Charlie.

Ethel couldn't take it. She became tongue-tied and red-faced. She moved her chair a few inches away from Charlie, and stared down at her beer, periodically bursting into nervous giggles. Finally, while Charlie was up getting another round of beers, Ethel just took off with Deke.

Charlie pretended he couldn't care less. For a while we sat around talking about what he was going to do with his life. College was out; the Gilhooleys barely afforded their weekly supply of SpaghettiOs, beer and gunshot. Charlie said he'd hate leaving Seaville but he'd have to, because there was no way he could ever be anybody in Seaville.

"It is a real pity that you chose to make yourself conspicuous," said Harriet.

"I don't mind being conspicuous," Charlie said, "I mind being poor."

"This town is dying," I said, and Harriet said, "Then we can't complain, honey."

While Harriet and I danced, Charlie sat by himself nursing a draft beer. "I hate to leave him sitting there alone," I said, and Harriet said, "I hope he won't go early and leave us without transportation."

Harriet watched over the money as though we were already married.

"A taxi will cost us four dollars!" she shouted across the floor at me while we did the boogie. "My father can't come and get us tonight, either. Hector has one car and Harvey has the other!"

"I've got the four dollars, Harriet!"

"Then we won't have enough to get hot dogs at Dunn's later!" Harriet complained.

"Let's not go to Dunn's tonight," I said.

"Oh, Wally!" She gave me one of her looks, because Dunn's was the place where everyone went at the end of a Saturday night, and Harriet was a girl who went to the place where everyone went at the end of a Saturday night.

"Where's all *your* money then?" I said. Harriet was the cotton-candy maker afternoons at the Seaville Soda Shoppe, but her salary was never part of "our" money, as mine was.

"You know I'm saving for my trousseau," she said. "You know Daddy's got to spend his savings on my brothers' educations."

We began having what Harriet liked to call later "a tiff" right there on the dance floor. It wasn't that I wanted her to spend her money. It was just that the whole idea of Harriet's trousseau sent me off into fantasies of shipping out for any destination on tramp steamers and banana boats. A year away didn't seem a lot like a year away when all Harriet seemed to do was talk about our wedding as though it was tomorrow. Out of all of Seaville High School, why had I picked the one Junior Ms. with antediluvian ideas like becoming engaged and saving for a trousseau? Charlie said it was because I was on the rebound and desperate, that when he'd been on the rebound from Bulldog Shorr he'd sent away for "So You Want to Be a Priest," published by The Junior Jesuit Society. ("How can you be on the rebound from somebody you were never even with?" I argued. "Try it sometime," he said. "It hurts worse.")

The set ended and the bandleader said, "Ladies and gentlemen, we have a celebrity in our midst this evening! Miss Sabra St. Amour! Tell me more, honey! Stand up and tell us more!"

"Don't tell me *she's* here?" Harriet said. "She must be slumming."

"*We're* here," I said.

"We don't have anyplace else to go," said Harriet. "We don't make forty to forty-five thou a year and could go anywhere in the world."

They threw a spotlight on her and she stood up in this pale yellow pants suit with her yellow hair spilling past her shoulders. She was smiling, and now there was no doubt who she was: She was made up; she looked the way she did on the tube, confident and beautiful, tossing out kisses through her fingertips while the piano player and the saxophonist tried to work out a few bars of her theme song.

It was Harriet's idea to get me to go over and ask her for a dance. I'm not sure whether Harriet wanted to impress other people with the fact I'd met her, or whether she wanted to sit out a set with Charlie so he wouldn't leave us without wheels.

Sabra introduced me to her mother, first, and her mother wanted to know how we knew each other. How in hell we knew each other. Mrs. St. Amour was this husky-voiced, big blonde with a bright red chiffon scarf tied around her neck. She was holding a long gold cigarette holder with one hand, a long, brown, unlighted cigarette attached to it. With her other hand she slapped her thigh hard and said at the top of her lungs, "Get this! She's got friends out here I don't know anything about!"

"We met briefly on the beach the other day," Sabra said.

"So briefly you didn't even think to mention it, hah?" her mother said. "Okay, little Miss Keep Things to Yourself! What are you, a closet extrovert?" She slapped her thigh again and laughed very hard at her own joke. Then she grabbed my hand, gave it a squeeze, pointed her cigarette holder at the man beside her and said, "This is Mr. Orr."

"Glad to know you, Witherspoon," he said.

"You're the kid from Current Events," said the man wearing "Am I Glad I Married Pearl Cohen!" He turned to his wife and said, "Pearlie, this is the kid who printed my shirt."

"You put the P on crooked," she said.

"Get up and dance, Sabra," said Mr. Orr. He had rust-colored, tight curly hair, and a shirt the same color. He was stirring a swizzle stick around in his scotch, smiling up at me.

"Would you mind?" I asked him.

Mrs. St. Amour gave my arm a punch. "I'm the one you ask that."

"Is it all right?"

"Have her in by nine o'clock tomorrow morning," Mrs. St. Amour said and let out a hoot. "No, no," she said, "you have my permission. You're a nice young man, aren't you?"

"I'm a nice young man," I agreed. Sabra was already on her feet.

I could feel everyone watching us. I could hear Mrs. St. Amour shouting, "They met on the beach! That's news to her mother!"

"Is Mr. Orr the one who gave you the gold bracelet?" I said.

"Do I look desperate?" she said.

I was imagining Lauralei Rabinowitz and Maury Posner sitting at a table getting an eyeful of me with her, even though experience and common sense told me that anyone who knew Lauralei Rabinowitz for less than three months was somewhere down in the dunes with a blanket, murmuring "I love you, I love you" into her soft black hair.

"Lamont's out here on business," Sabra said. "He's a writer for our show."

"Then who did give you the bracelet?" I said.

"Someone wonderful," she said.

"Oh I know him," I said.

Way back by our table I could see Harriet and Charlie standing on chairs so they could get a better look at us. Every few seconds someone glided past us and purred "Tell me more."

"I suppose this happens to you a lot," I said.

"I don't go out a lot," she said. "The only thing that happens to me is the neighborhood hand laundry asks for an autographed picture, to put up beside the sign that says 'Not responsible for articles of clothing left after thirty days.'"

"If you don't go out a lot, what do you do a lot?"

"Work," she said. "I work a lot."

Duffo Buttman, one of the Seaville High quarterbacks, stopped us so he could get Sabra's autograph on his lobster bib. "Just say 'To remember a dynamite evening,'" he said, handing her a Pentel.

After she signed the bib for him, she asked me, "What do you do a lot?"

"I go to school a lot."

"College?"

"First grade," I said.

"I just finished high school," she said. "I don't know if I'm going to take any college courses or not. What are you going to do when you get out of first grade?"

Myra Tuttle and Louise Rand appeared with paper napkins and a ball-point pen. "Just say 'Loved seeing you,'" Myra said.

Louise said, "You can say something like 'Good luck, Louise.'"

I stood there grateful that they'd come along and interrupted the conversation. I knew where the conversation was leading. It was leading right toward BEAMS.

My father is a Son of Beams. He has a black-and-white cap up in our attic with SONBEAM stitched across it. Everyone in my father's family for generations has gone to BEAMS. BEAMS is the reason my Uncle Albert ran off to join the Navy, age seventeen.

Albert is my father's older brother. He went from the Navy to working as an apprentice printer, to teaching dancing at Arthur Murray, to managing a McDonald's, to teaching canoe at a boy's camp in the Adirondacks, to exterminating rats in Chicago, to playing at a roadhouse and living in a trailer camp. My mother calls him The Flop of the Two Families, and Uncle Albert signs all his postcards and letters "No regrets, Albert."

"Everybody makes jokes about BEAMS"—my father had variations on the same remarks five or six times a year—"but I'll bet Albert would give his right arm to be able to do it all over again and go to BEAMS."

"I doubt that Albert could do it all over again without his right arm," I said.

"Don't *always* wisecrack, Wallace," said my father. "I enjoy a good joke or two myself about the profession. Why when we get together at conventions, you should hear the kidding around that goes on. We have picnics with Casket Casseroles and all that sort of thing. But I'm trying to tell you where Albert made his mistake."

"He always signs his mail 'No regrets,'" I'd point out. "It doesn't sound like he thinks he made a mistake."

"People who have no regrets don't have to sign things 'No regrets,'" said my father. "Do I sign things 'Happily married and settled down?' I know what Albert's life is like. No security. Living in a trailer camp with the kind of people who live in trailer camps. Albert's been all the way around the world and he ends up playing 'Blue Moon' in a roadhouse and calling a trailer home. Do you know why?"

"He didn't want to be an undertaker," I said.

"A man without a profession is a man without more than about two hundred dollars in savings his whole life."

"Maybe Uncle Albert doesn't want a big savings account," I said.

"So long as his health lasts, maybe he doesn't," said my father. "But what about the day sugar shows up in his urine, or the old ticker gives out, hmmmm? Both things run in the Witherspoon family. Albert ran out on his old age when he ran away those many years ago. He spit in the face of Fate."

Fate, for the Witherspoons, according to my father (and my mother), is BEAMS.

BEAMS is Broadhurst Embalming and Mortician School.

"If you were ever so foolish as to consider running out on your old age," my father always added, "I hope you'd realize that you'd be running out on me, your mother, Ann Elizabeth, the whole family, its tradition and its livelihood."

Sabra finished autographing and turned back to me. "What were we talking about?" she said.

"I don't remember," I lied.

"I remember. We were talking about what you were going to study after you got out of first grade."

"It's too early to know," I said.

"I knew what I was going to be since I was old enough to walk," said Sabra.

"Some people are just lucky that way," I said.

That was the point when Harriet sent Charlie over to cut in.

When I got back to the table, Harriet said, "Who's the couple she's with?"

"Her mother and a writer for the show," I said. "Did we look stupid dancing?"

"Good," she said. "You didn't look any more stupid than you used to look when Lauralei Rabinowitz towered over you."

"Thanks a bunch," I said. "Why did you say good?"

"Charlie's going to ask her to join us," Harriet said. "We'll save four dollars."

10. Sabra St. Amour

When Charlie asked me to join them, I shook my head and rolled my eyes to the heavens and said Mama would just never hear of it. I said if Mama had her way I'd have tattoos all over me saying "Fragile," "Keep Your Distance" and "No Trespassers." Charlie persisted, saying I was almost old enough to drink, vote and get married, and I kept replying, "You don't know Mama!"

By the time Charlie asked Mama, all the Chartreuse she'd been drinking must have caught up with her. "I think that's a swell idea," she said. "Why not? You go ahead, honey. Charlie, you see that she gets home safely, hear?"

I leaned down and whispered to Mama, "I can't stick you with Lamont."

"I'm going to ditch him at The Seaville Inn in about ten minutes," said Mama. "Then I'm going to sit out on the deck and watch the moon with my old pals Frankie and Perry and Tony and Andy, while they sing to me."

Lamont pretended to cut something with an imaginary pair of scissors.

When I asked him what he was doing he said he was cutting the umbilical cord.

I don't know why I ever started discussing Lamont's stupid play when we got to Dunn's Drive-In. If the leading critic for The *New York Times* reviewed it with nothing more than a series of Z's, why did I think I was going to come off any better telling Charlie, Wally and Her the plot? (Right from the start I sensed that I was going to have trouble with Her.) I was nervous, that was part of the reason I started on it. The only kids I'd ever been around were kids like me, who went to Professional Children's School in Manhattan.

I know you've probably all read and heard interviews with kids who do what I do for a living, either on T.V. or in the movies. There's always a line in those interviews about "offstage little Blah Blah is just another youngster, no different from other children." If you believe that, you believe that rain is dry and the sun is wet. All of us little Blah Blahs are about as much like ordinary kids as Volkswagens are like Rolls-Royces. Ordinary kids don't have agents who take ten percent of their earnings; shrinks who charge fifty dollars an hour to listen to their problems; wardrobe people who help them dress and undress; makeup people who hide their blemishes; and fans who try to telephone them, write them, wire them and send them everything from chocolate layer cakes to bus tickets to Cincinnati. Most of us little Blah Blahs have huge scrapbooks, too, filled with press clippings.

Mama was my agent and my manager, so I was different from some kids: We kept it all in the family. But sometimes I wondered what it would be like to have one of those mothers you see on soaps or series who come out of the kitchen in an apron, asking how your school day went and warning you to wash up for dinner because it'd be served at six-on-the-dot. Those kind of mothers never spill green liqueurs down their cleavage, then call for another round in a loud voice, waving a fifty-dollar bill.

I suppose when we got to Dunn's, I was trying too hard to act like just another normal teenager without having a clue what that really meant. There was a strong wind blowing, too, as we parked beside the other cars at Dunn's, and that was the way Lamont's play began, with this enormous wind.

I've known a lot of gay actors, so it was easy being with Charlie. I knew he was gay without anyone telling me because Charlie was the type we'd say came out of the closet without even a hanger trailing after him. He was all the way out. It was Wally and Her I was having trouble with. Wally had this defensive, wise-guy pose that made me want to forget I'd ever asked him to go to a movie with me, and She was what Mama would call a bitty and a half. When I got in the Fiat while we were leaving The Surf Club, She said you must be having a divine time seeing how the other half lives, and when I said you've got me all wrong, I hardly know how *anyone* lives, She said in this snide tone, "Tell me more."

The moment I started on *The Wind of Reluctant Admissions*, I had the feeling there was a balloon over Her head with SNORE written inside it, and Wally kept acting as though he was afraid of what I was going to say because of what it would inspire Her to say back.

"Okay." Charlie finally took over and tried to sum up what I was describing. "There's a mythical kingdom somewhere, and when the wind blows very strong like this wind tonight, people have to make reluctant admissions."

"You have to admit whatever's on your mind," I said, wishing I'd never started the whole thing.

"Reluctant Admission," She said. "This game is stupid."

"Oh you're sweet," Wally said to Her. "You're known for it."

"Reluctant Admission," She said. "I'd like more mustard."

Charlie bit into his hot dog. Then he said, "Reluctant Admission."

"Well?" Wally said.

"I was going to try and make out with Easy Ethel tonight."

"Reluctant Admission," Wally said. "I'm a full-blooded Cherokee Indian."

"I *was*," Charlie said. "I thought I could use the experience."

"Use it for what?" She said.

I bit into my hot dog. Then I said, "Reluctant Admission."

"What is it?" Charlie said.

"I'm going to send back this hot dog," I said. "It tastes like a piece of cooked inner tube."

"They're always like this," She said. "This is the sticks."

"They're always awful," Wally agreed.

"They're just tacky old Dunn hot dogs," She said, eating hers with more enthusiasm than ever.

"It wouldn't do any good to send it back," said Charlie.

"I always send something back when it's terrible," I said. I got that from Mama. Mama likes to say if you give your best you have a right to expect the best, and you should never settle for less. Mama is always sending something back: forks because there's a spot on them; rolls because they're not warm; whipped cream because it's not real; salad dressing because it's bottled; orange juice because it's not squeezed fresh. Mama says an important lesson is never be had, by anyone!

Harriet said, "What do you eat in New York City at the end of an evening?"

"That depends on where we go," I said. "If we go to the Brasserie, I order onion soup with the thick cheese crust. Or quiche Lorraine. If we go someplace like the Algonquin, I order chicken crepes."

"This must be a real downer for you," Harriet said.

"I just wouldn't pay for it," I said.

"Charlie's paying for it," She said.

"*Harriet!*" Wally said.

"Send it back, Charlie," Harriet said.

"Drop it, Harriet," Wally said.

"Would you like me to get you something else?" Charlie asked me.

"Forget it," I said. "It doesn't matter."

"Reluctant Admission," Harriet said. "We're fresh out of quiche Lorraine and chicken crepes. How about a sour pickle?"

"Their hamburgers aren't too bad," Charlie said.

"I'm not really hungry, anyway," I said.

"A dollar and a quarter later she tells us," Harriet said.

"A dollar and a quarter for these?" I said. "Hey, let me treat," and I reached for my purse. Mama had shoved two tens at me just before I left the table.

Charlie put his hand down on mine. "Don't," he said gently.

"Let her if she wants to," Harriet said. "She won't ex-actly have to pawn her fancy gold bracelet."

"My, how the time passes when you're having fun," Wally said.

"When does curfew ring tonight, Harriet?" Charlie said.

"One o'clock as usual, Charlie," She said. "We won't have time to make the Algonquin, I fear, what a pity! . . . Reluctant Admission: One o'clock won't come soon enough where I'm concerned."

All the way to Harriet's house, She and Wally didn't talk. Charlie made small talk compulsively, the way Fedora runs off at the mouth on the set, when an actor does something to displease her and she can't wait to get him alone and chew him out. Fedora always keeps up appearances, while she's seething inside.

Harriet didn't bother saying good night. She ran ahead of Wally while he was walking Her to the door.

"She's just jealous," he said when he climbed back into the back seat.

"Of what?" I said. "Of me?"

"Of everything," Wally said. "Of you because she doesn't have dates who pass out thick gold bracelets, or send back her food because it's terrible, or take her to the Algonquit for quiche Lorraine."

"The *Algonquin*," I said, "for chicken crepes."

"The Waldorf Astoria," Charlie said, "for creamed caviar over smashed brains."

"The Astor," Wally said, "for stuffed rooster under plexiglass."

"The Paris Continental," I said, "for asses' ears in green sauce."

"Waiter!" Wally said. "Take back this aardvark nose, it's running."

"Garçon!" Charlie said. "Remove this camel's eye, it's crying."

It was my idea that the evening shouldn't end. Charlie and Wally and I were just beginning to loosen up and laugh, and I didn't want them to remember me as this spoiled Superstar-Creep who told old play plots in detail and wanted to send back a Dunn's hot dog because it tasted like a piece of cooked inner tube.

"Nightcaps at my place!" I sang out, the way Mama always invited people back to our place at the end of an evening. On the way I told them how Lamont came to visit our apartment in The Dakota and called it a lovely little *pied-à-terre*. I told them how we called him Lamont Bore on the set, and how he did this little dance of rage when anybody changed his lines, like old newsreel clips of Hitler's jig of joy when Germany invaded another country.

I didn't tell them anything about my ulcer. I doubted very much they knew many kids their age with ulcers; I didn't want to come off that far out or neurotic. I might have been able to tell Charlie about it because I had the feeling I could tell him anything, but there was something really laid back about Wally, where I was concerned. He seemed to answer all my questions with some wisecrack; I got the feeling he thought I thought I was Miss Grand from Videoland.

I suppose my shrink would point out that I didn't have anything to fear from Charlie because he was gay. My shrink didn't do a lot of pointing out—they don't, they mostly listen, which is why analysis goes on for years—but she wasn't above hinting at the fact that my infatuations were with fantasy figures; I never let myself get involved with anyone who could threaten me. Threaten me! I'd say; yes, threaten you, she'd reply: *Move* you. I'd quoted Bette Davis once: "You can't have a career *and* a love life." Dr. Mannerheim said, "Wasn't she married several times, though?" (If you know anyone who's ever won an argument with a shrink, send me her name. I'd like to frame it.)

"Congratulations on not smoking for the whole evening!" Wally said as we roared down Ocean Road toward the beach house.

"Congratulations on not knocking Harriet Hren's teeth down her throat," said Charlie.

"That, too," Wally said.

"I've given up vice and violence," I said.

"When are you going to give up men who pass out expensive gold bracelets?" Wally said.

"Will you forget the man who gave me that gold bracelet?" I said.

"If you will, I will," he said.

"Oh it sounds like love," said Charlie.

Mama had forgotten to put on the outside light, so Charlie had to get his flashlight out of the glove compartment. He went first, shining the light back on the wooden steps we had to climb to get up to the beach house. I was in the middle, with Wally behind me.

We were halfway to the top when I heard Tony Bennett's voice singing the song about having left his heart in San Francisco.

"Mama's playing all her old tapes again," I said.

"Do you have any old Beatles tapes?" Wally asked.

"We're like Sam Goody's record shop," I said. "Do you ever go to Sam Goody's?"

"In New York?" Wally asked.

"They've got everything," I said.

"We should have brought some beer," Wally said.

"We have beer," I said. "What kind of a bar do you think we run?" I sounded a lot like Mama when people came by. Mama prided herself on having anything anyone asked for, from pink gin to Tia Maria. She said when she was a kid her father kept one bottle of blackberry brandy that would last practically an entire year. If a guest came, he'd pour a thimbleful into an old Kraft Olive Pimento jar, and never give anyone a refill.

Charlie turned around at the top of the stairs.

"Is the screen door locked?" I said.

He started down.

"Call Mama," I said, "she's probably out on the deck."

He put his hands on my shoulder and very firmly turned me around. "She's not out on the deck," he said.

"Then she's gone to bed," I said, "and left the tape on."

"They're in the living room," Charlie said. "Let's go for a walk on the beach."

We left our shoes up in the dunes and rolled up our pant legs. We walked all the way to the next town on the hard-packed sand by the surf. I don't remember what exactly we talked about, but it wasn't anything to do with Mama and Lamont. We didn't mention that once.

We were laughing and everything, but I couldn't tell you what at. I had this knot beginning in my stomach that told me I'd be swallowing down liquid Maalox until the sun came up.

I took deep breaths of the salt air and tried to remember everything I'd ever learned in a Yoga class I'd once taken, to calm me down. I kept repeating "Chee chee," which was my own secret mantra from the Transcendental Meditation course Mama and I had paid seventy-five dollars apiece for, and I said to myself, "Damn you, Mama," over and over, too, which made me feel better than anything.

On the way back practically all the lights were out in the large mansions overlooking the Atlantic. We watched the ones in the little beach houses go off. We passed some kids lying on blankets in the sand, and sitting around a campfire drinking beer.

"Hel-lo, Wally. Hel-lo, Charlie," some girl called out.

"Hello, Myra," Wally said.

"Why Myra Tuttle," Charlie said, "I thought you were a *nice* girl."

"Oh tell me *more!*" she screeched.

When the house Mama and I were renting came into view, there were a lot of lights on, including the outside ones. The wind was blowing up harder as we trudged up to the dunes to collect our shoes, whipping the sand against our faces.

Charlie said, "Reluctant Admission."

"I hope it's really gross," Wally said.

"I couldn't have made out with Easy Ethel if she had stayed with me. That was just macho talk, that was just a phony lie."

"I don't think you missed much," Wally said.

"Reluctant Admission," I said. "Mama gave me that

cuff bracelet. I've never even been on a date."

"Now that *is* gross," Wally said.

"Tonight's my first night out. . . ever," I said.

"Welcome out," Charlie said.

"Oh all right," Wally said. "Reluctant Admission. This is for you, Sabra."

"Don't talk so fast," I said, "I don't want to miss this."

"Well?" Charlie said.

"Well?" I said.

"I lied when I said I didn't know what I was going to be," Wally said. "What I'm going to be is an undertaker."

"Oh *that*," Charlie said.

11. Wallace Witherspoon, Jr.

Sunday my father had to drive to the Hauppauge morgue to pick up a new guest. That left Mr. Trumble and me to put the caskets back in the Selection Room. This is the room where relatives come to pick out the coffin and finalize the financial arrangements for a funeral.

My father got the idea to do ours over because of an article in *The Knell*. That's a monthly magazine published by The American Funeral Directors' Association. According to the article, the Selection Room was the most important one in a mortuary. It could make the difference between a funeral selling for under a thousand dollars and one going for three thousand or more, depending on lighting, decor and ambiance. (On the front cover of *The Knell*, there is an hourglass with the sand running out.)

Our Selection Room had just been newly wallpapered with violet fleurs-de-lys on a white background. While the interior decorating had been going on, the caskets were stacked in the garage. Mr. Trumble and I had to lug them back in and arrange them so that the expensive ones were in prominent positions under the lights.

Mr. Trumble's face was turning the color of the inside of a watermelon, and sweat was trickling down his forehead into his bushy white eyebrows.

"I hear you been dating a movie star, Wally," he said.

"I haven't been *dating* her," I said. "She's a television star, Mr. Trumble."

"You always had fancy notions, Wally."

"Don't try to talk, Mr. Trumble," I said. "Let's get this stuff moved first."

"You afraid I'm going to slip my cable on you?" he said.

"What?"

"You afraid I'll get my sailing orders and leave you to fill my shoes?"

"There's no sense pushing your luck, Mr. Trumble," I said.

"You go from girl to girl like a grasshopper, Wally," said Mr. Trumble. "Well, make hay while the sun shines."

That night I dreamed that Sabra St. Amour and I were flying high in the sky like two birds, floating, falling, touching. Then out of her mouth came Lauralei Rabinowitz' voice: "Don't touch my legs, Wally. I need a shave."

Monday morning Mrs. St. Amour called to ask if I knew where Sabra was. I answered the phone in our Memory Chapel. I was helping my mother prepare for a service the following evening. Our new guest was old Mrs. Wheatley, who'd been teaching history at Seaville High for twenty-five years, living with her mother until her mother became our guest last year. A.E. was searching for Gorilla, who'd been napping with Miss Wheatley until my mother walked into Slumber Room I and began screaming, "What are you doing in there, Gorilla! A.E., get your cat out of here!"

Mr. Llewellyn, our organist, was practicing two pieces Miss Wheatley had requested for her memorial service:

"High Hopes" and "Tell Mother I'll Be There." He was singing "High Hopes" when I took Mrs. St. Amour's call. Every few seconds he'd trill "Whoops! There goes another rubber tree—Whoops! There goes another rubber tree plant!"

"If you don't know where she is, maybe your friend Charlie does," said Mrs. St. Amour. "What's Charlie's last name?"

"Gilhooley," I said.

"If you should see Sabra, tell her Lamont's gone," said Mrs. St. Amour. "Can you remember that?"

My mother finally said to Mr. Llewellyn, "Matthew, are you supposed to sing, or simply play the tune?"

"I'm supposed to sing, Miriam, according to her last wishes. She liked the words to the song."

"It's a very inappropriate song for a memorial service, if you ask me," my mother said.

"Not for Miss Wheatley's memorial service," I said. "She always had RISE ABOVE IT written in large letters behind her, on the blackboard."

"Matthew," said my mother, "would you mind practicing later this afternoon? I'd like to have some private words with my son."

Mr. Llewellyn nodded and gathered up his sheet music.

"Why does Sabra St. Amour's mother think you know where her daughter is?" my mother asked me.

"Charlie and I are the only ones Sabra knows out here," I said.

"And Charlie doesn't count," said my mother.

"Why doesn't he count? He counts," I said.

"Not when somebody's looking for her daughter," said

my mother. "I hope you're not getting into something, Wally."

"I'm sorry I mentioned anything at all about Sabra," I said. "Now everyone in Seaville will know it after you go to the hairdresser this afternoon."

"I don't gossip," said my mother, who was second only to Mr. Jim of Mr. Jim's Beauty Salon in the Seaville Gossip Department. "How long do you think your father would last in his profession if I was a gossip?"

"Dead men tell no tales," I said.

"Neither do I," said my mother. "Do this woman and her daughter plan to leave after Labor Day?"

"The light over the lectern has burned out," I said. "We'll need a replacement."

"Not that I give a hoot about either one of them," said my mother. "Even poor old Miss Wheatley was probably happier all her life than they've been for one month of theirs."

"Miss Wheatley was stuck in Seaville and she knew it," I said.

"Miss Wheatley taught you history. Period," said my mother. "You knew nothing about her personal life."

"She didn't have one," I said. "Everybody in Seaville knew she didn't have one, thanks to her mother."

"Then why would she request 'Tell Mother I'll Be There,'" said my mother.

"Irony," I said. "I think she was being ironical."

"Miss Wheatley?" my mother said.

"Miss Wheatley," I said.

"Pffft!" my mother said. "Miss Wheatley ironical."

"Her whole message was to overcome, to strive," I said.

"Behind RISE ABOVE IT there were all sorts of other slogans. 'He who limps is still walking.' 'Many strokes overthrow the tallest oaks.' On and on."

My mother said, "I think you're reading your own ideas into hers."

"I'm going into the kitchen to look for a bulb for the lectern," I said.

"Someday ask your new, famous friend how much security she has," said my mother.

"Security isn't everything," I said. "Convicts are secure, so are dogs tied to trees."

"I just hope you don't talk that way around your father," said my mother. "Where will we all be if he has a severe attack before you're ready to take over for him?"

"He knows how I feel already," I said.

"And he's been very patient with you, Wally," she said, "because he went through a period when he felt some reluctance, too, right after Albert skipped out."

"Some reluctance?" I said. "I don't feel some reluctance. I feel a lot of reluctance! I feel one-hundred-percent reluctant!"

"Tell *me* about it then. Don't tell him about it!"

"I'm telling you right now," I said.

"Why do you want to get on this subject this morning?" my mother said. "Don't you realize I played bridge with Ruthie Wheatley? We sang in the choir together. She was like a sister to me."

"Mother, you hardly knew her."

"Don't be heartless, Wally," said my mother. "I have very strong feelings about nearly all of our guests. The tears were streaming down my cheeks when I worked on

Ruthie. Your father can verify that."

"I give up," I said, which was exactly what my mother wanted me to do.

A.E. was giving Gorilla a lecture in the kitchen. "You're going to wind up in the A.S.P.C.A., Gorilla," she was telling the cat as she brushed her. "You won't sleep on satin over there."

"Where are the light bulbs for the lectern?" I asked her.

"They're in the utility cabinet where they always are," A.E. said. "There's a letter for you on the bread box. It was hand-delivered a few minutes ago by Hector Hren."

I picked up the envelope with my name on it, in Harriet's handwriting. Harriet made circles over her o's with little faces inside them.

"Love leaves me weak, I cannot speak," said A.E. "Emily Dickinson wrote that. And if my words do leak, from pent-up heart, I start, I sneak, to say your name."

"Take mother a light bulb for the lectern, will you?" I said. "Please?"

"What do you think of that poem?"

"It's fine," I said, ripping open the envelope.

"Do you really like it?"

"I said it's fine."

"Well Emily Dickinson didn't write it," A.E. said. "Your very own sister wrote it."

"*Dear Wally*," Harriet's letter began. "*When I offered to loan you a hundred dollars ($100) toward the ring, you said nothing.*"

"If you say Emily Dickinson wrote it, or Sylvia Plath wrote it, or Edna St. Vincent Millay wrote it," A.E. said, "everyone swoons over it. If you say you wrote it, you get screwed."

I said, "You better take the hand vacuum and touch up around Miss Wheatley. Visiting hours start in fifteen minutes."

"This is a business like any other business," A.E. imitated my mother's voice. Then she fell to the floor spread-eagled with her eyes staring straight ahead and her mouth hanging open.

Gorilla jumped down from the kitchen stool she was perched on, walked over A.E.'s stomach, strolled down the ramp and headed back toward the Slumber Rooms.

"Oh no you don't!" A.E. was on her feet, scrambling after her.

> . . . *You may think a ring old-fashioned but as the ads say a diamond is forever and why should I promise my self to you for nothing? My father has an old saying that goes "What we obtain too easily we esteem too lightly," so think that one over, Wally. Another thing is the way you treated me when we got to Dunn's Saturday night, as though the special one was the great afternoon actress and not yours truly. I would also be curious to know what you were doing walking on the beach with her much later, which you needn't bother denying since Myra Tuttle saw you there with her own eyes. Oh sure Charlie was there too for your front! Sometimes I think you are really lower than a worm.*

I couldn't read beyond the word "worm." Every time I saw the word "worm" I remembered all the times I'd answered the phone and heard some kid singing, "The worms crawl in, the worms crawl out, they crawl up and down your dirty snout." Then laughter and a click.

Whenever A.E. got jokers like that on the telephone, she always sang back, "We'll be seeing you, before you know it!"

"Ann Elizabeth," my mother would tell her, "if that happens again, simply say, 'You are an ill person and you should see a doctor.'"

One night A.E. told one of the jokers, "You are an ill person and you should see a doctor." We were all sitting around the dining-room table while A.E. took the call, and my mother had this pleased expression on her face, because A.E. for once, seemed to be carrying out my mother's instructions. Then A.E. said, "And after you die from your illness, we'll be seeing you!"

When I got to Current Events that afternoon, Martha was chewing out the lending-library man because all the novels he'd supplies were years old.

"I'm a laughingstock," Martha told him. "Who's going to pay fifteen cents a day to take out old books like *Jaws* and *Once Is Not Enough*?"

"Monty told me to concentrate on nonfiction," said the man.

"Monty's an ass!" Martha shouted. "Are you the last one in Suffolk County to find out Monty's an ass?" Then she began to cry and the lending-library man put his arm around her and said the humidity was getting to everyone, they should go somewhere for a cool drink.

"You'll mind the store, won't you, kid?" he asked me.

Martha said, "There's just one shirt order, Wally.

It's pinned on the bulletin board next to a message from Charlie Gilhooley."

Martha got her bag from behind the counter and they started out the door. "I'm only doing this work because I was laid off from my regular job," the lending-library man was saying. "What I am is a lathe operator down near Commack."

I unpinned the shirt order and the message from Charlie. Someone named Sussman wanted a shirt with "Wink if you want a sex change" printed on it. Charlie's message was *Please buy me an inexpensive backgammon game and show up at my house around four. S. is coming.*

12. Sabra St. Amour

Saturday night when I got back from my walk on the beach, Mama's bedroom door was closed. Lamont was washing brandy snifters in the kitchen. He had a dish towel stuck in the V of his baby blue cashmere sweater to protect it, and another one stuck in his belt to protect the front of his white linen trousers.

"Did you have a good time?" he said, as I walked in carrying my shoes. He smiled over his shoulder at me as though nothing had happened.

"We had a dynamite time, Lamont, particularly when we came back here about an hour ago."

"Don't give your mother a bad time about that, Sabra," he said. "We both had too much to drink."

"Don't tell me how to handle Mama," I said. I lit the first cigarette I'd had since I met Wally. "Why are you hanging around here?"

"I didn't know I needed a reservation at The Seaville Inn. They're full."

"I bet you didn't know you needed a reservation," I said.

"You've got to accept the fact your mother's an attractive woman," he said. "She was intended to be something more in life than your personal slave."

"Was she intended to be your personal bankroll?" I

said. "You're saving yourself forty-five dollars a night staying here, and I bet Mama bought all the drinks at The Surf Club."

"It's none of your business who bought the drinks," he said. "Nobody has to answer to you, Sabra."

"You're never going to get near a storyline of mine," I said. "I'll never say a word you write!" I was actually hissing through my teeth at him.

Then I went into the bathroom and got sick.

When I came out, the door to the guest room was shut and Mama's door was open. She was standing there in her bright orange robe with the white boa fringe, holding her head with one hand, blinking at me. "Are you all right, honey?"

"Go to bed, Mama," I said. "I'll be fine."

I felt a little punch of disappointment when she did. It was the first time I'd ever been ill that Mama hadn't tucked me in.

Sunday mornings Mama never made an appearance until after Dr. Robert Schuller's sermon on television. He was this little blue-eyed, bespectacled man who preached positive thinking while the cameras swept around the church showing thoughtful faces, flower arrangements, then trees outside, fountains and people sitting in parked cars listening to him. A lot of the times I'd crawl in bed with Mama and watch, too. Mama and I did a lot of things like that together. Sometimes we'd fix a huge bowl of buttered popcorn and watch Lawrence Welk in bed, or we'd find an old Metro-Goldwyn-Mayer musical extravaganza and make a fried chicken/potato salad picnic to eat on the floor in front of the set while we watched.

Lamont drove into Seaville to avoid another confrontation with me, to get The *New York Times* and have breakfast. I made Mama her hangover cure: skimmed milk with a tablespoon of brewer's yeast and a tablespoon of wheat germ, whipped up in the blender. Then I took it in to her. I figured she'd have the guilts pretty badly and I didn't want her to. All I wanted her to do was tell me Lamont was going, for good.

"Are you feeling better?" I asked her.

"Are you?"

"I didn't think you'd remember that I was sick last night," I said.

"Oh I remember," Mama said. "I remember last night very well."

"I took some Maalox and it helped," I said.

"I'm glad something did," she said. "Maggie, I'm sorry if you were embarrassed in front of your new friends, but that's life."

"I thought it was gross and juvenile," I said. "I think they did, too."

"Well juveniles don't have a corner on gross and juvenile behavior," said Mama. "You kids think we're supposed to pack it all away the day you're old enough to answer back."

"I can see getting smashed," I said. "I wouldn't mind if he was someone your own age."

"I wouldn't mind that, either," said Mama. "Open the windows wider, please, Maggie. I could use some fresh air."

I went across and pulled the drapes and fixed the windows. Then I went back and sat on the edge of Mama's bed. "Mama," I said, "what if I decide not to go along with this new storyline of Fedora's?"

Mama's expression didn't even change. "What if you do? The last thing I want to talk about right now is storylines."

"You may not ever have to again," I threatened, "if I quit for good."

"That's right," Mama said.

"Do you really hear me?" I insisted. "I'm talking about giving up my career for good. *For good.* I want to go to college." That last sentence was a surprise even to me.

"I hear you," Mama said. "Turn on channel 9. *Hour of Power* is coming on."

That afternoon I stayed in my room while Lamont read Mama's tarot cards out on the deck. I could hear Lamont forecasting a possible trip and a meeting with a dark stranger, and Mama squealing and exclaiming, while I turned the pages of a book I wasn't even reading. I was still in my room when they went swimming, and later when Mama came in and asked me if I wanted to go out to dinner with them.

"I'm having spasms," I lied. "How could I eat?"

"Rest and take your Librax," Mama said. "We won't be late."

Monday morning early, I took off in the Mercedes without leaving any note. I drove to Hampton, bought a copy of *Daytime TV* and had breakfast in a luncheonette there.

There was a feature article in the magazine called "Sabra and I Have to Wait." It was supposed to be an interview with Peter Tripp, the daytime actor I'd gone to the awards banquet with almost a year ago and never seen since. Peter played a preacher's son who was always in trouble, on *Turning Point*. He was fifteen and when he wasn't in front of a camera he took out his contact lenses and wore thick Coke-bottle-bottom glasses, scratched his eczema, and played some game of his own invention called "Where Is?" (Where Is Fels Planetarium?. . . Wrong! It's in Philadelphia! Where is Nakhon Si Thamarat? . . . Wrong! It's in Thailand!)

There was a picture of me out in front of the studio, and a picture of Peter, with his lenses in and his Airedale on a leash, and a quote which was supposed to be Peter's, in a banner over the two pictures. "We knew what was happening to us and why it couldn't be!"

The writer of the article probably never even met Peter. He probably wrote the story from notes he'd taken down during a telephone conversation with *Turning Point's* publicity person.

The article was about our magic attraction to each other and how we had to fight against it because of our careers. Peter was supposed to have promised his dead twin brother he'd be a star by the time he was twenty-one, because that had been his brother's ambition. "*Sabra,*" the article continued, "*would never do anything to upset the dream, for in real life Sabra is a deeply sensitive girl who wants to grow professionally as much as she wants Peter to realize his ambition. But there are long nights, too many of them, when their hearts ache for each other.*"

It was a bad, dated picture of me, taken way back when the Wedge was in style (my hair hasn't been that short in years), and I made a mental note to find out if *Hometown's* publicity department was still sending out photos like that, or if it had come from an old file of the magazine's.

After I finished breakfast, some vacationers on the main street spotted me, and I signed a few autographs.

Then I shopped and kept calling Charlie's until he came home.

That afternoon on *Hometown*, Storybook Sabra had a scene with her shrink as the tune-in-tomorrow tease at the end of the show. Charlie and Wally and I watched it in Charlie's living room, while Charlie and I played backgammon.

Storybook Sabra had been trying to fit in to a normal life at Clear City High School, after her mother's indictment for murder. She was telling her shrink about her experience with a sorority that had been rushing her.

> **Sabra:** I didn't make Tri Ep.
> **Dr. Day:** Do you blame your mother?
> **Sabra:** Not really. I knew they wouldn't pledge me, even if Mom wasn't up on a murder rap. I'm not like them.
> **Dr. Day:** Is that the only reason you think they don't you?
> **Sabra:** Isn't that always the only reason people don't want you? It's why they don't love you, too. All the cliques in the world from sororities to churches to kaffeeklatches to your own relatives are saying just one thing: I'll love you when you're more like me.

There was a slow fadeout on my face with tears glistening in my eyes. The tears were actually drops of Visine.

"That's a neat line," Wally said. "I'll love you when

you're more like me. That's really what my father is saying to me underneath it all."

"It's what the whole world is saying to me," Charlie said. "Sabra, I think I'm going to gammon you."

"Your game," I said, picking up my pieces. "I'll never make it."

Mama'd say that Charlie's house was kitschy. It was as far from the feeling in our apartment in New York as a cactus plant growing out of a china turtle's shell is from a bonsai tree. There were plastic slipcovers on the rayon slipcovers. There was a yellow vinyl recliner with a magazine pocket stuffed with old copies of *Gun World*. There was a machine-made sampler framed on the wall that said: RELIGION SHOULD BE OUR STEERING WHEEL, NOT OUR SPARE TIRE. There were two miniature American flags crossed under a picture of Charlie's father as a sailor in World War II, on the mantel beside a stuffed owl. There was wall-to-wall yellow carpeting with a floral pattern and a deer's head hanging out from the wall over the T.V. In one corner there was a glass gun case with a padlock on the door. In the opposite corner there was a very green and shiny-leafed plastic palm tree.

Charlie's mother was helping run a yard sale, so we had the house to ourselves. When I'd arrived there, I'd called Mama.

"Okay, Maggie, where in the name of blue blazes have you been? I called the hospitals."

"At a friend's house."

"Whose?"

"Mama, I have my private life and you have yours."

"Mine has left for New York," said Mama.

"I don't care where Lamont is," I said.

"I told him you want to leave the show for good, so there's no point in his hanging around Seaville. How's your tummy?"

"I'm sure you've got more pressing matters to worry about," I said.

"Are you taking Librax?"

"Like how to spend more money on Lamont," I said.

"Lamont is gone, Maggie. Now come home. We'll have dinner and compose a letter to Fedora."

"I'll be home for dinner," I said.

"I want you to know you're doing the right thing, too."

"By coming home for dinner?"

"By leaving *Hometown*," said Mama.

After *Hometown* went off, Charlie and Wally and I lazed around watching a *Batman* rerun. I hadn't done anything like that since The Dark Ages when Sam, Sam, Superman had us trapped in suburbia and I was under the spell of Elvis Presley. Mama called what we were doing "lollygagging." She'd come bursting into my room, turn off Elvis and say to me, "What are we doing lollygagging around here like Mrs. Average and her daughter, Mediocre? Let's go to The Apple for some fun!"

We'd head down the Palisades Parkway for New York doing eighty. We'd visit agents and casting directors Mama'd known when she was in the business. Mama would show me off and brag how well Sam, Sam, Superman was doing, exaggerating like crazy. (He was working for Tackier Brothers Toy Company then, pushing Adam Zee Worm, a computerized animal that said the alphabet, and One, Two, Three Flea, another one that counted to a hundred and lived on a plastic dog's back.)

My own father had been an actor like Mama, only he hadn't lived long enough to make a name for himself. "It's in your blood, Maggie," Mama used to tell me. "You're not just another salami decorating the deli ceiling—you're special!"

We'd end up someplace like the Promenade Cafe in Rockefeller Center for their Summer Sundae; Joe Allen's for pecan pie; or the Russian Tea Room for baba au rhum. Mama could always turn an ordinary day into something different; neither Mama nor I were ordinary-day types.

I was thinking a lot about that while the three of us hung around Charlie's. A part of me was standing over by the gun case sizing up the scene, and wondering how I'd fit in anywhere without *Hometown*. Until I'd talked to Mama on the phone that afternoon, everything I'd said about quitting the show had a make-believe feeling to it, because I'd really just been threatening Mama with the idea. There was nothing make-believe about Mama's tone of voice, though.

Charlie was talking about some new idea his father had to send him out to Oconto, Nebraska, to work on a farm. An old Navy buddy raised cattle someplace in Nebraska, and needed more hands.

"Maybe you'd like it," Wally said.

"Maybe I'd *hate* it," Charlie said. "I never even heard of Oconto, Nebraska."

"Don't do anything you don't want to do," I said.

"My father says I can't hang around here, it's not a boarding school," Charlie said. "My job at Loude's ends in September."

"Why Nebraska, though?" Wally said. "It's so far away."

"That's why," said Charlie.

"You should go to New York City," I said. "You'd fit in there."

"My mother thinks it's Sin City," said Charlie.

"Nobody gives a hoot if you're gay in New York," I said.

"If I told my mother I was going to New York City to live, she'd have to take all the dirty pots and pans out of the oven where she shoves them, so she could put her head in and end it all. Once a week my mother spends a whole day taking a Brillo pad to every pot and pan we own. They stack up in there until it looks like a Teflon graveyard."

"You want to know something my shrink says?" I said. "She says the solutions to all your problems are right in front of you, waiting to be handled. They're like horses with the reins already attached to them. It's just up to you whether you want to grab hold of the reins." If *my* shrink ever said anything that long she'd have to go to bed for a month to recover from complete exhaustion. It was really something Dr. Day, Storybook Sabra's shrink, had said.

"What would I do in New York?" Charlie said.

"Get a job. Meet me for coffee after my classes."

"Where are your classes?" Wally said.

"I don't know yet, but I'm grabbing the reins. I'm quitting the show."

"*Why?*" Wally said.

"I'm going to be a normal person," I said.

"I can't stand overachievers," Charlie said.

At that point Mrs. Gilhooley came through the back door calling out, "Charles? Are you in there? I need some help with a cornucopia I bought you for your room at the yard sale!"

"How did you know I always wanted a cornucopia for my room?" he said.

"Don't be so smart, this has got the waxed fruit already in it," she called back, "and it's a knockout!"

Before I drove home, I dropped Wally off at his house.

"Would you go out sometime with me?" he said.

"You mean now that I'm going to be a normal person?"

"You have to start somewhere," he said.

"Sure," I said, "call me."

13. Wallace Witherspoon, Jr.

Late Monday night, Legs Youngerhouse, the tennis pro at the Hadefield Club, was shot to death by a jealous husband. Tuesday morning we were busy preparing Slumber Room II for him, at the same time getting ready for Miss Wheatley's funeral. When my father discovered we were short one pallbearer for Miss Wheatley, he told me to call Charlie and see if he could get a few hours off from Loude's.

"For eight dollars an hour, I'll carry Legs on my back all by myself," said Charlie. "I'm going to need all the money I can get my hands on by Labor Day."

"It's not Legs you'll be carrying, it's Miss Wheatley," I said, "and I thought you'd be more upset."

"I got over Legs a long time ago," Charlie said.

Mr. Llewellyn was practicing "High Hopes" again in our chapel. My father and Mr. Trumble were backing out the ambulance to rush down to the Hauppauge morgue for Legs' body.

Charlie said, "I broke the news last night that I'm going to New York."

"You can tell me about it when you get here," I said. "You'll need a dark suit, white shirt, quiet-type tie."

"There's not much to tell," Charlie said. "My mother wept until the nine-o'clock movie came on, and my father said if I wanted to live in a big city I should consider San Francisco."

"Why San Francisco?"

"I think because it's farther away," said Charlie. "Are suede shoes okay?"

"As long as they're dark," I said.

While I was dusting the coffins in the Selection Room, Deke Slade called to say they hadn't received a single order from any of Legs' family or friends.

"It isn't a P.O., is it?" he asked.

"Not that we know about," I said.

"By the way, I'm having a party Thursday night," he said. "Eight o'clock, if you want to come."

"Thanks," I said. "All the red roses you sent over for Miss Wheatley are dead already."

"Then bury them with her," Deke said.

In addition to "Evasions," I wrote one other composition for English that Mr. Sponzini gave me an A+ on. It was called "Fear and Funerals," and it was about all the superstitions responsible for the way we bury the dead.

I spent a week researching it at the Seaville Free Library. I started off by knocking down the theory that the wearing of black had something to do with showing respect for the dead. The truth was that mourners wore black originally out of fear that the ghost of the corpse would want to lure them to their deaths, too: Black was thought to be an inconspicuous color that wouldn't call attention to those nearest the coffin.

The coffin was carried out feet first so the corpse couldn't look back and beckon one of the family to follow it in death. The long, exaggerated eulogies were because no one wanted to chance offending the dead. The flowers were to appease the ghost; the music was supposed to lay his spirit to rest, and so was the handful of dirt tossed into the open grave.

"What are you proving, Wally?" my father said when I showed him the composition.

"I'm not proving anything, just explaining how these things came to be," I said.

"It seemed to me you're knocking the business," said my father. "I don't care if you did get an A+. Don't bite the hand that feeds you."

As a curious man, on the scale of one to ten, my father rates about −1 when it comes to the folklore of funerals. Although he'd never own up to it, I think he still carries with him a lot of the old guilt undertakers used to have about the profession. Some of them actually used to live in towns miles away from their mortuaries, and pretend they were commuting shopkeepers or salesmen.

You might call my father a bland conversationalist. He likes to make small talk about weather record highs and lows, anyone's family connections, a ballplayer's batting average, or anything that falls into the category The Way Things Were Back When. He and Mr. Trumble can do a whole number on the hurricane of '38, Pearl Harbor Day, or butter rationing during World War II. There's no radio back in the shop. The two of them reminisce while they work. You can turn on the intercom that connects the shop with our house and hear them:

"Wasn't she Louise Waite's niece?"

"Oh yes, a Waite on one side and a Palmer on the other. You can see the Palmer resemblance."

"Well Louie was a holder of the Purple Heart, if I remember correctly."

"It was the Congressional Medal of Honor, Mr. Trumble. Purple Hearts weren't that rare, you know. Artie Young got one, lot of boys did."

I was always forgetting my father's aversion to certain types of information. There was a famous philosopher, I don't remember which one, who said the unexamined life was not worth living. My father seemed to feel the examined life wasn't. The afternoon of Miss Wheatley's funeral I was reminded again of how he felt. Three of Miss Wheatley's faculty friends from Seaville High had sent three large orchids with a card attached which said, "*Ruthie, we'll be with you before long: Gladys, Gert and Frances.*"

Charlie was riding in the flower car with Mr. Trumble, who was feeling tired from the trip to Hauppauge. I was riding in the hearse beside my father. My father's a very thin, tall man who looks a little timid because he has a habit of backing away from people when he talks to them, and because he wears these rimless glasses that went out of style in my grandfather's time. Both the backing away and the glasses are part of the undertaker's syndrome: I mustn't offend. The glasses, he believes, are the least offensive and conspicuous. I think he backs away out of fear his breath might smell. My father's always asking me or my mother to "okay my breath."

He was driving along with the lights of the hearse on, although it was a bright, sunny afternoon. I think funeral processions look weird going along with the lights on in the daytime, but then again if it didn't look weird, it wouldn't be much like a funeral procession, because anything to do with funerals is far out.

My father was talking business per usual, and per usual I was trying to tune him out. He was telling me that he was working on old Mr. Sigh to make "prearrangements" for his sister's and his funerals, adding that the Witherspoon Funeral Home "heretofore" hadn't paid sufficient attention to the very practical idea of recommending prearrangements.

"When grief's in the way, it's hard to impress on a customer the necessity of a truly memorable send-off," my father was saying. "And half the time the type coffin they might choose is out of stock; they settle for less, regret it all the rest of their days. . . . Then too, some old folks like Mr. Sigh don't even know if anyone who cares about them will be around when they pass. Those important details are left up to strangers." That was about when I interrupted.

"I'll bet Gladys, Gert and Frances would have second thoughts about sending orchids if they knew the word 'orchid' meant 'testicle.' "

"What are you talking about, Wally?" said my father.

"The word 'orchid,'" I said. "It means 'testicle.'"

I saw a nerve jump at the side of his face.

I said, "*Mirabilis est orchis herba, sive serapias, gemina radice testiculis simili.*"

"Is that Italian?" said my father. "What are you talking about?"

"That's Latin," I said. "Pliny the Elder said that. He was this famous Roman naturalist, and what he was saying was that the orchid was remarkable because with its double roots, it resembles the testicles."

My father drew a deep breath, blinked, let it out. He looked at me sharply, briefly, then back at the road.

"Wally, I'm going to give you a tip," he said.

"What's that?"

"That is that children say everything that comes to mind but adults do not. If I said everything that came to my mind, where do you think I'd be in this business?"

The idea of my father blurting out something gross fascinated me.

"Give me an example," I said.

"An example of what?"

"Of something that could come to your mind that you'd be better off keeping to yourself."

"There's no necessity for an example," said my father.

"I'm just curious about what comes to your mind," I said.

"You're too curious about most everything," he said.

My father didn't say anything for a while. The hearse turned down Cemetery Road, the cars behind us in the procession winding around in the same direction like a long black snake with headlights for eyes.

Then my father said, "I have my thoughts. You think I don't, but I have them."

I wished we weren't so near the cemetery because I was warming to the subject.

"Are they ever bad thoughts?" I said.

"Why would I have bad thoughts?" he said. "Your thought about the orchid was not a bad thought. It was an inappropriate thought."

"It's appropriate for a naturalist, or a linguist or an etymologist," I said.

"None of which you are or I am," said my father.

"Mr. Sponzini said I'd be a good linguist or etymologist," I said.

"I doubt that Mr. Sponzini makes fifteen thousand dollars a year," said my father.

"Isn't that a little off the subject?" I said.

"He's hardly someone to give advice," said my father. "Wally, your remark about the orchid and its alleged meaning calls to mind the time you brought up the word 'lust' at the dinner table, when we had Reverend Monroe for rib roast. You were going for the shock effect."

"I was not," I lied. "I thought it might interest him that 'lust' meant pleasure once, until everyone decided that pleasure was sinful. He laughed, didn't he?"

"It's one of his duties to be politic," said my father, "but he and I and your mother would have preferred not to have had the subject of sex brought up while we were eating. He barely finished grace before you leaped to introduce it."

I remembered something I'd presented Lauralei Rabinowitz with right after I met her, before I'd talked her into examining the inside of a hearse back in our garage. It was a piece of white construction paper with a red heart pasted on it. Across the heart I'd written out a quotation I'd copied down from an old book I'd once found behind the other books in my father's library. The name of the book was *On Life and Sex: Essays of Love and Virtue*, by Havelock Ellis. The quotation said:

> *The sexual embrace can only be compared with music and with prayer.*

I'd put this in a large manila envelope decorated with other hearts and tied with a red ribbon. I'd passed it across to Lauralei in the cafeteria.

Late that same afternoon she walked by my locker and handed me an envelope with my name written across it in fancy script. The envelope was sealed with red wax and PERSONAL was printed across the back.

Inside was a carefully printed message:

WALLY, YOU ARE SO FULL OF B.S. IT HURTS!

"In our business," my father continued as we glided toward the cemetery in our air-conditioned Cadillac hearse, "we pride ourselves on staying in the background, and I don't necessarily mean physically. I mean that we're discreet. We don't feel compelled to step forward and spout off the things we know. We're privy to many mysteries and secrets. Wally, you're not in our business long before you know an awful lot about your neighbors."

I became involved in an instant daydream of Sabra St. Amour running toward me on a hill, the wind blowing her hair behind her, her arms outstretched.

"Sometimes a bruise on the body tells you something," said my father.

We were laughing and stumbling toward each other.

"The fingernails tell you something," said my father.

We were slipping, falling on soft grass, holding each other.

"The hair, the soles of the feet," said my father.

We were rolling down the hill together.

"The hands," said my father.

We stopped, we lay there close together and she whispered something with her lips touching my ear lightly: *Grab the reins.*

"Believe me," said my father, "our business is chuck full of privileged information, Wally."

What I said next surprised even me. "Don't call it our business anymore, Dad. I've made up my mind that I won't go to BEAMS. I want to go to college." I'd said it very fast, but very distinctly.

We could see the cemetery coming into view. That same nerve jumped at the side of his face. He gripped the steering wheel harder. I could see his knuckles turn white.

Then, almost like the passing of a seizure, he untensed, looked sideways at me with his quick, minimal smile and said, "I thought you might feel that way, Wally. I felt that coming."

"I want to go to college," I repeated.

We were turning into the cemetery. "You may," he said.

"I *can*?"

"BEAMS can wait," my father said.

I almost felt Miss Wheatley prod me from behind us, and I shouted then: "BEAMS IS OUT!"

We pulled to a stop a few feet away from her freshly dug grave.

14. Sabra St. Amour

"Here's one from the Princeton freshman again," said Mama. "He starts off 'My Beloved Sabra.' His folks are wasting their money sending him to college." Mama was sitting out on the deck with me, in her bathing suit, with her reading glasses slipping down her nose, poring through a box of fan mail with me.

"Why do you think they're wasting their money? He sounds intelligent," I said. I was in my suit, too, helping Mama devour a box of Mallomars. Except for the one slip that Saturday night, I was still not smoking. I was eating instead. Mama was doing both, not bothering to sneak smokes anymore. She was chain-smoking.

"Somebody in college watching soaps?" Mama said. "He should be reading Socrates or something. Shakespeare, John Wadsworth Longfellow."

"Henry Wadsworth Longfellow," I said.

"Henry, John—he should be getting an education." Ever since Fedora invented the "Tell me more" gimmick, I'd been getting about two hundred fan letters a week. Some of the fans seemed to believe what was happening to me on the tube was happening to me in real life. I got advice, proposals of marriage, invitations to parties, criticism and questions on every subject from how I felt about abortions to how someone got a job on the soap. (I also got threatening letters and obscene ones, which Mama kept in a file in case anything ever happened to me.) I answered some of the mail myself; some Mama answered, and a lot of it went to a part-time secretary who sent back a standard "Thank you for your interest" letter, and my photograph which she signed my name to.

Mama wasn't quite her old self. She jumped whenever the telephone rang. She had her prescription for Valium refilled at the Seaville Rexall.

Monday night when I got home for dinner, Mama had fixed a Rochambeau omelette like the ones we loved to have at a little restaurant in New York called Madame Romaine de Lyon. She said we'd work on the letter to Fedora over the weekend, that Lamont would probably give her the news, anyway, when he got back to New York.

"Poor Lamont," I said. "He'll have to con his way in somewhere else."

"Lamont's not desperate for work," Mama said. "He's up for a Guggenheim grant and he's up for a grant from The Ford Foundation."

"Being up for a grant isn't getting a grant," I said.

"Plus his agent says his new musical is another *My Fair Lady*."

"Mama, I can't *believe* you're taking Lamont seriously, suddenly!"

"Who's taking him seriously?" said Mama. "He's another Leo, like Sam was, only worse because Gemini's rising."

"He's another loser like Sam was, only worse because he's a taker," I said.

"So?" Mama said. "I'm a giver. Where would a giver be without a taker?"

"Mama, just a while ago you were bad-mouthing him to Fedora!"

"Just a while ago I was a young bride. Just a while ago I was a young widow. Just a while ago I was a bride again. Just a while ago I was a widow again. Don't tell me about just a while ago," Mama said.

"But Lamont is the pits, Mama!"

Mama just shrugged and we dropped the subject. Mama and I almost never fight. We bicker and snipe at each other, but we never have the fireworks she used to go through with Sam, Sam, Superman. I remember once when I was little, I got Mama to take me for an audition at K.K.B.&O. advertising agency, for a small part in a butter commercial. They wanted a pudgy little girl, which I was. We'd heard about it on one of our excursions to The Apple, while Mama was traipsing around showing me off to her casting-director friends. When Sam, Sam found out about it, he threw all Mama's shoes out on the front lawn—it looked like it had rained shoes for a week. He just went ape before our eyes, yelling that no stepdaughter of his was going to turn into a butter saleswoman so Mama could make our house into a shoestore! I tried to get in between them to tell Sam, Sam it had been my idea, not Mama's, but he picked me up bodily and dumped me on my bed in my room. He said if I came out he'd tie me up and gag me.

I could hear Mama screaming, "You're no respecter of talent, Sam!"

"Talent doesn't dress up like a bar of butter and dance around on top of a slice of bread!" Sam, Sam shouted back.

"Talent doesn't sing sick little ditties about 'Sun yellow butter is better butter, ask my mutter!'"

I stood beside Mama crying as hard as she did at Sam, Sam's funeral, but I wasn't crying because he was dead. I was crying because Mama was crying, and it always scared me when Mama got out of control. I could almost always, all my life, make Mama laugh, or change her mind about something, or go places and do things with me, but for a while after his death, I couldn't reach her. The day of the funeral she kept saying over and over, "No one in this whole crummy world ever loved me like Sam did!" and she'd just look through me like I wasn't there when I'd protest that I did, I loved her more.

After we sorted through my fan mail, Mama read me a long memo from Fedora that had arrived that morning. It said that the whole cast of *Hometown* was in agreement about staying a half-hour show, if it meant keeping me.

Of course we will stick to our plan to use Sabra off camera in as many scenes as possible, with voiceover letters from her, reveries with still shots and telephone calls. I am, in fact, right now developing an extremely exciting storyline concerning Sabra's flight from the cruel incidents of the sorority turndown, etc., in Clear City, to her older sister's home in Seattle, where she will become involved with a fanatic religious group like the Moon organization. Her ulcer will heal, but she will need to be rescued. This theme will begin to appear late this year and carry over into the fall of next year.

"See what you're *not* missing?" Mama said.
"I'd be a dynamite Moonie, though," I said.

"You'll be a dynamite college graduate," said Mama.

"I'll major in John Wadsworth Longfellow," I said.

"Oh har har har de har har," Mama said. "So they never taught Longfellow before the eighth grade, which was when yours truly split."

"You did okay," I said.

"I did hah? Do you call doing okay not being able to think of a bigger word than 'stupid' during a Scrabble game? That's why I hate Scrabble."

The telephone rang then and Mama knocked the Mallomars box off the deck scrambling to answer it. But it was just Charlie Gilhooley telling me he'd like to come by that afternoon to talk about some kind of dance contest Seaville held every summer.

"I hope you're not expecting to hear from Lamont again," I said. "That's really gross."

"I see you've picked up a new word," Mama said. "Who wrote it for you?"

Charlie was there about an hour before Mama suddenly got up from the redwood chaise where she'd been pretending to read *Variety* but really listening to us talk. She was still wearing her pink-and-white latex bathing suit, which was tight on her because she'd gained weight as I had; she had on rope-soled platform clogs, with her reading glasses hung around her neck on a gold chain.

"I've got an idea," she said, turning down the Jack Jones tape. "I happen to know a dance nobody will remember that'll put that contest on its ear!"

Mama looked down at her feet and hummed to herself for a minute, then she started doing steps. "This is a dance from the thirties," Mama said, "when I was little enough to come to about your knees, Charlie. I was in London, just getting started in vaudeville, when vaudeville was just petering out. I don't like to think I contributed to its demise." Mama put her hands on her hips and laughed. Then she started doing more steps. "Da da da da dee dee dee," she sang, moving in time with the rhythm, "deedle daddle daddle dee—me and my gal, doin' the Lambeth Walk!" She put one thumb over her shoulder as though she was hitch-hiking and called out, "Hey!"

She said, "You either yell 'Hey' or 'Oi' at the end, I can't remember."

I looked at my watch. I said, "We're on in a few minutes, Mama." Mama never missed *Hometown*, even if I wasn't on it that day.

"This was in a fantastic show called *Me and My Gal*," Mama said. "It was the hit of all England. Everyone was doing this Lambeth Walk. It's like a walk, too, I mean you practically walk. Get up here, Charlie, and I'll show you."

"Mama," I said, "it's almost four thirty. The scene where I visit my mother in prison is coming up."

"You want to watch it, watch it," said Mama.

"Me?" I said. "I hate myself on tape."

"Charlie?" Mama said.

"That show was in 1938," Charlie said, getting up from his chair, joining Mama in the center of the deck.

"Let's hear it for the boy genius," Mama said. "Now follow me, Charlie: daddle daddle deedle dee, daddle daddle—no, your left foot points out."

"Daddle daddle deedle dee," Charlie said, doing steps.

"Deedle deedle daddle da," Mama said.

"Me and my gal," Charlie sang.

"Doin' the Lambeth Walk!" they both finished. "Hey!"

The phone rang again.

The smile on Mama's face wilted. She was balancing herself on one foot, watching me while I reached over to the windowsill to pick the arm off the cradle.

"I'm just about to become part of a funeral cortege," Wally said.

Mama was making who is it with her lips.

I waved my hand at her and pointed to myself.

"It's a little dead around here, too," I said.

"There's a party tonight. Would you like to go?"

"You and Harriet and Charlie and me?"

"You and me," he said.

"Oh," I said.

"You have to start somewhere. Remember?"

"What'll I wear?" I said.

"Jeans," he said. "Eight o'clock."

"Is it for dinner?"

"At eight o'clock?" he said.

After I hung up, Mama said, "Is Wally coming by?"

"We're going to a party," I said. "Tonight."

"He told his father he isn't going to be an undertaker," Charlie said. "I hear his father's barely speaking to him."

"Is that okay with you, Mama?" I said.

"Is what okay with me, that Wally's father doesn't speak to him?"

"Is it okay with you for me to go out with him tonight?" I said.

"Honey, you're a big girl now," Mama said. Then she said to Charlie, "Watch my feet carefully."

I looked at my watch again. It was four forty-five. For

the first time in my memory, *Hometown* was on, I was in it, and we weren't watching.

"Daddle daddle deedle dee," Mama started up again.

"Deedle deedle daddle da—" said Charlie.

I thought of a line one of the sorority girls in Clear City said about being asked for her first date: "I felt as though finally *I* was beginning, after so long of wondering if there was a real me somewhere."

That was the way I'd felt when I went for my first audition. I thought about that and ate the rest of the Mallomars.

15. Wallace Witherspoon, Jr.

At the cemetery, while the mourners gathered around Legs' open grave, I sat in the hearse trying to answer Harriet's latest communication. Hector Hren had hand-delivered it to our house that morning. It was in response to a telephone conversation I'd had the night before with Harriet.

There were the usual black smudges on the paper. Harriet always made carbon copies. Even when she scribbled a quick note in class telling me she'd expect me at eight o'clock that night, she slipped carbon under it to preserve a duplicate. All of them were filed under Witherspoon with my answers, numbered and dated. Harriet said her mother had done the same thing when Harriet's father was courting her. For their first wedding anniversary, Mrs. Hren had organized them all into a leather-bound scrapbook; on the front in gold were the words *Remember, Remember!*

While Reverend Monroe began the prayers, I reread what Harriet had written:

> *Dear Wally,*
>
> *We could have made a real go of the Witherspoon Funeral Home, but that's beside the point. (I even thought of naming the Slumber Rooms. It seems so impersonal to have them I, II and III. I thought of The Adieu Room, The Au Revoir and The Arrivederci.) I*

think you are letting a good thing slip through your fingers because your head is turned by a certain Prize Narcissus and I don't mean the flower.

I am not going to wait while you go to college and figure out what you do want to be. I would be Tuenty-two. My mother was married when she was nineteen, and had the ring already for a year.

Hector is right, you will never find someone like me again who is interested in helping the man she marries, as my mother helps my father. (I would have liked to create a special room for guests under eighteen. Death among the young is becoming even more common, par-ticularly suicide: Statistics will bear me out on this.)

Wally, in a rash moment (I hope) you have smashed a family tradition and bro-ken your father's heart. Who is he to turn to now to entrust with his family's future security?

If you could do something like this to him, what could you do. to the one you asked to be your bride?

Okay, maybe you will change your mind, and then (if it is not too late) I will consider taking up where we left off, but for now I must say we can't see each other anymore, and the engagement is off.

Here is something my father likes to quote from the famous George Bernard Shaw, since you are so fascinated by words and sayings: "When a prisoner (which you claim you've been, Wally) sees the door of his dungeon open, he dashes for it without stopping to think where he shall get his dinner outside." Think about it!

So Wally, good luck if you really mean what you

said, but count me out. (I would, however, be interested in knowing if this is a definite decision.)
    Sincerely (I mean that!),
    Harriet

    P.S. Any ideas included herewith for the Witherspoon Funeral Home may be used if so desired. (I had a lot more, too!) HH.

My letter back to Harriet reminded me of the one Lauralei Rabinowitz had written me after she began wearing Maury Posner's bar mitzvah ring around her neck and wanted me to stop calling ten times a night to hear her voice and hanging up. You know the kind of letter I mean, all about how you still respect the person and would really like to remain friends, blah blah blah blah, but while you felt love you weren't in love, blah blah, and although you wouldn't trade the memories of the two of you together for anything in the world (except Maury Posner, I told myself bitterly when I read Lauralei's little masterpiece), this was the end. "*The definite end*," I wrote, "*to us and to my ever considering being an undertaker again.* (I'll find someplace to get my dinner outside, don't worry.)

    And so, Harriet, adieu, au revoir, and arrivederci! WW."

I'd no sooner finished than someone from the Seaville American Legion stepped up to Legs' grave with a trumpet and played taps. The woman Legs had been playing around with (her husband was being held without bail) dropped a bouquet of white roses from Slade Florist into the open grave, and Legs' mother lifted the veil from her own face and spat at her. My father moved up behind Mrs.

Youngerhouse with his hands fidgeting nervously, while Reverend Monroe called for another prayer. There was no further incident.

On the way back from the graveyard, my father rode with Mr. Trumble, who was diminished and feeble looking behind the wheel of the flower car. I parked the hearse in front of the Hrens' with the motor running, and left the letter for Harriet with little Hedy Hren. Then I stopped off at Current Events to print up a shirt for Sabra saying "Grab the Reins!"

I expected Monty to make some crack about the fact I'd parked the hearse outside his store. Monty was putting in September issues of magazines and pulling out Augusts that hadn't sold. Martha and Lunch were nowhere in sight.

I said, "Don't tell me you're minding the store for a change?" I grabbed a black, small T-shirt, and picked out silver letters to steam onto it.

"Hello, Wally," said Monty (I think it was the first time he'd ever just called me by name, without interjecting some insult, which gave you an idea of his bad mood). "How goes it?"

"Okay," I said. "Are you all right?"

"Am *I* all right?"

"Yes."

"Why wouldn't I be all right?" Monty said. He didn't wait for an answer. He slammed some old August *Town & Countrys* on the floor and said, "You can't tell her to stop ordering ten of these things a month. I've been telling her that for six years and she goes right on ordering ten of these things a month!"

I positioned the letters and plugged in the steam press.

"Let him learn for himself," Monty was muttering.

"Are you talking about me?"

"I'm talking about him. Have you seen him?"

"Who?"

"Some jackass lathe operator," Monty said. "She's having coffee with some moronic lathe operator who totes lending-library books around in his spare time."

I held the press down and watched the minute timer. "I haven't seen him lately," I said.

"He must have a lot of brains if he's falling for Martha," Monty said.

I didn't hang around to hear more. All my mother needed to hear was that our hearse was parked on Main Street while I fooled around in Current Events. Things were bad enough around our house without that.

The night before at dinner I felt as though I was eating at Monty and Martha's. My father kept saying to my mother or A.E., "Ask him to pass the salt," or "Tell him I'd like the butter." He refused to say my name or direct any conversation to me. To make matters worse, he'd received a postcard from Uncle Albert that day, which he read aloud at the table.

No longer entertaining at Hiz 'N Herz. (You can't win them all.) Moving along to Florida for the winter, where I'll be holed up at The Sunny Haven Motel. Could use about ten sawbucks until I accept another position, whereupon I'll scoot them right back to you. Well, how's everything with you and the folks? No regrets, Albert.

"You can't win them all," my father said. "How many times has Albert written to say you can't win them all!"

"Ten sawbucks, my *eye*!" said my mother.

"What's a sawbuck?" A.E. asked.

"A sawbuck is a ten-dollar bill," said my father. "Asking for money embarrasses Albert, as it should, so he resorts to slang."

"All he's ever done with his life is resort to," said my mother.

"That's right," said my father enthusiastically. "He resorts to this job, he resorts to that place to live. A rolling stone gathers no moss and no roots. Of course certain people at this table aren't particularly interested in roots, anyway."

"I'm interested in roots," I said, "but I'd like to be able to put them down myself."

"Certain people," said my father, "believe that old, established professions are to be scoffed at."

"Linguistics is an old, established profession," I said. "So is semantics. So is plain old journalism. I'm not scoffing at them."

"Are you going to send Uncle Albert the ten sawbucks?" A.E. asked.

"Certainly not," said my father, who would; we all knew it.

That night my father didn't even come to the table. He had pains, my mother said. He was resting in his room. "Another thing," said my mother. "Adelade Hren called me a while ago to say that Harriet is a complete wreck because of some letter you wrote her. Adelade wanted to know if I knew what was in that letter, and I told her I had no idea you'd even written Harriet a letter."

"It doesn't have anything to do with Mrs. Hren and you," I said.

"I just hope it wasn't a Dear John," said my mother. "I wrote a Dear John to someone during the war and to this day I think about it at night when I can't sleep. It's something I'll always regret doing." In our house there was only one war, which was World War II.

A.E. said, "Is a Dear John a letter saying you don't love someone anymore?"

"I never really loved this particular person," said my mother.

"Then why did you write him a Dear John?" A.E. said.

"*Because,* Ann Elizabeth, I *imagined* that I loved him," said my mother.

A.E. said, " 'After all, my erstwhile dear,/My no longer cherished,/Need we say it was not love,/Just because it perished?' Edna St. Vincent Millay."

"A.E.," I said, "stop quoting yourself and saying it's Edna St. Vincent Millay."

"That really was her," A.E. said. "If I could write like that, would I be sitting around this dinner table wasting my time worrying over what's going on in your dull life?"

"Your brother's life isn't dull, A.E.," said my mother. "Uncle Albert's is a lot duller."

"What does his life have to do with mine?" I asked.

"You're thinking of imitating him, aren't you?" my mother said.

"I'm not thinking of teaching canoe at a boy's camp, or

teaching dancing at Arthur Murray, or exterminating rats, or playing piano in a roadhouse. I'm thinking of going to college and doing something with words."

"Well you've just done something with words," said my mother. "You've dashed your father's fondest hopes with words, and apparently you've done something with words to poor Harriet Hren."

"You're off to a brilliant start," said A.E.

Since we had no guests in the house, my mother had made pork chops and home fries with extra onions. I could still taste the onions after I'd showered and brushed my teeth and dressed, so I went back down the hall to the bathroom to try mouthwash.

My father was sitting in his room with the shades pulled down, no light but the one from the television. He was watching a ball game, his leather recliner in the third position, a glass of skimmed milk on the table next to him. My father usually shut the door when he watched television upstairs, but the door was open that night to make a point, to tell me I was responsible for the shape he was in.

He finally called out to me, "Wallace?"

I went to the door and looked in at him. He was still wearing the trousers he'd worn to the funeral, a white shirt and dark tie, but his shoelaces were untied. He began cleaning his glasses with the edge of his fresh white handkerchief; it was easier for him to talk with me when he didn't see my face clearly.

"What is it, Dad?"

"Tell your mother to put on the Ansafone. I don't feel up to taking calls directly right this moment."

"All right," I said. I lingered a moment to see if he'd say anything else.

He finally said, "Is it the girl, Wallace?"

I stepped inside the room a little more. He kept cleaning his glasses, not looking up at me. "It isn't the girl," I said. "Her name is Sabra, by the way."

"Your mother and I are well aware of her name." He sighed.

Then he shook his head. "She's just passing time at the end of the summer, Wallace." He blew on his glasses. "She's turning your life around, and all she's doing is passing time at the end of a summer."

"It isn't Sabra," I said.

"I'll be lucky if Mr. Trumble lasts through fall." He didn't put his glasses back on after he finished cleaning them. He held them by one of the arms and swung them slightly. "It seems to me you're burning all your bridges behind you, Wally."

"Maybe that's what you have to do if you don't want to go back over old ground again," I said.

"The Hren girl was one in a million," said my father.

"Well she still is, for someone else."

My father put his glasses down beside his milk and put his hand up near his heart.

"Are you all right, Dad?"

"Oh I'll be all right."

"I can help out around here," I said. "I still have another year of high school."

"*If* you even finish," he said. He shut his eyes.

"Are you sure you'll be all right?"

"I'll be fine," he said.

"What do you mean if I finish? I have to finish."

"I'm beginning to realize you don't believe you have to do anything."

"I have to finish high school to go on to college."

"I have to find a way to afford it, I suppose," said my father. "If anything happens to Mr. Trumble, I'll have to sell out, Wally, or let someone buy in."

"I'll look into scholarships," I said.

"I don't want to talk about it anymore," he said. "A girl comes along and *pffft*, you don't listen to reason. I knew you took them in the hearses but I never said anything."

"Dad, it isn't the girl. I just don't want to be in this business."

"So you said," my father answered, "so you said. Now shut the door and go."

My mother was on the phone with Mrs. Trumble when I was ready to leave for Sabra's. I asked A.E. to tell me if there were onions on my breath. A.E. pretended to keel over from the stink. She was stretched out in the hall her usual way, with her eyes open and staring, her tongue hanging out, legs and arms apart and stiff.

"Ann Elizabeth!" my mother interrupted her telephone conversation long enough to call in. "I told you that you were never to do that again!"

A.E. got up and told me, "You'll be fine, really, if you just don't sit next to her, dance with her or talk to her."

"I want you to go right to your room, Ann Elizabeth," said my mother, "and stay there!"

"See how you've got everyone in a panic around here?" A.E. said. "Why can't you just accept the idea that the dead are no different from you or me, they're just in another stage of development." Then she moved stiffly down the hall, lumbering like Frankenstein's monster, her hands outstretched, face frozen in position, deep moans escaping from an exaggerated O-shaped mouth.

I bent over and kissed my mother's forehead while she was still on the phone.

"Try to keep him in bed, Mrs. Trumble," my mother was saying. "He should always rest between guests."

16. Sabra St. Amour

Mama said she had this colossal idea: She'd go out and buy all the makings for paella if Charlie would like to have dinner with her. Charlie said he didn't even know what paella was but he'd like to have dinner with her anyway. Mama said tonight's the night you learn all about Spanish food. She said they'd start with gazpacho, paella would be the main course, they'd end with flan, and wash it all down with sangria.

"And what'll I eat?" I said.

"You'll eat some roast chicken which I'll pick up for you," said Mama. "You'll have to eat earlier than us because of your party. *We* will dine at the fashionable Spanish dinner hour of around ten o'clock." Mama did a few fast flamenco steps, and pretended to click castanets in her hand. "How does that sound to you, Señor?"

"Olé," Charlie said.

Mama went charging off in the Mercedes to shop, and Charlie and I sat out on the deck playing backgammon.

"I hope you don't feel like you're stuck with Mama for the night," I said.

"I hope she doesn't feel like she's stuck with me," he said. "I really like your mother."

"That makes two of us," I said. "After you move to New York, you'll see a lot of us."

"*If* I move to New York," Charlie said.

"What do you mean if?"

"Why should I move to New York where I'll be mugged by some heroin addict, when I can live out here by the ocean?"

"Hey, don't get cold feet," I said. I remembered something Storybook Sabra had been told by her mother's best friend, Etta Lott, who'd been ostracized by everyone in Pine Bluff for having her baby without marrying or identifying the father. He was Pine Bluff's powerful mayor.

"Don't be afraid of what's new: It's the old, tried-and-true ways that should terrify you. Nothing creative, original or beautiful was ever begot by walking in step like everyone else. You have to step out of line to give the world something special."

"Well I have stepped out of line," Charlie said. "I don't know about giving the world something special."

"You'll do that in New York," I said. "New York will appreciate you."

"Will *I* appreciate New York, though?" Charlie said.

"Why are you even having second thoughts, Charlie? You said yourself your father wishes you'd go even farther away."

"Why should I live my life in a way that'll make him more comfortable?" Charlie said. "He never lived his to make mine more comfortable."

I became Etta Lott again. (It was funny: I couldn't even remember who'd played Etta on the show, but I could almost see her idiot cards cueing me.) "Don't find excuses to conform. Find excuses to excel."

"My father likes to say that if an ass goes traveling, he

doesn't arrive somewhere else a horse."

"Your father is typical of the great unwashed," I said. "That's a name we use for those members of our viewing audience in the sixty-to-seventy I.Q. range."

"I could excel here, is all I mean," Charlie said. "I don't know what at, though."

Etta Lott told him, "Take long steps and by all means look back. You'll see everything behind you getting smaller, and eventually passing completely out of view."

"I like the way you put things, Sabra," Charlie said.

Charlie beat me again in backgammon, then went down to take a swim. I bathed and washed my hair. I heard Mama when she came back, banging things around in the kitchen. When the phone rang, Mama called out "St. Amour residence!" Then I heard Mama talking in a low voice, for a long time. I went out into the hall and tried to make out what she was saying, but I couldn't hear her clearly. When my curiosity got the best of me, I pretended I'd picked up the phone in my room to make a call. Mama was talking to Bernadette Young, who did publicity for *Hometown* and was a friend of Mama's from the old days.

"Oh, and did you get my letter, Peg?"

"It came this morning."

"Is that you, Sabra?" Bernadette said.

"Sabra, are you on the extension?" Mama said.

"Be sure and tell her about the book," Bernadette said.

"I'm right here on the extension," I said.

"I'll tell her," Mama said.

"He'll only be in New York for twenty-four hours, Sabra," Bernadette said. "He's passing through on his way from Europe to the coast, and the idea just came to him."

"Who?" I said.

"Oh my God," Mama said, "I'll *give* her the message!"

"Milton Tanner is who," said Bernadette. "G'bye."

I hung up and ran downstairs with my hair still wet. "Mama, did Bernadette say Milton Tanner? *The* Milton Tanner?"

Mama was quartering a chicken. She'd fixed a tray for me with some chicken already cooked on it, and a glass of milk, cottage cheese and sliced tomato. "She mentioned his name, yes. Take your tray up."

"She more than mentioned his name, Mama," I said. "She said something about a book."

"Well that's what he is. He's a writer who writes books."

"I *know* he's a writer, Mama," I said. "I *know* Milton Tanner. He writes articles, too."

Everyone in the business knew him, although most of the people he wrote about weren't daytime stars. They were nighttime: stars of series and specials, and movie stars. Everybody in daytime has this big inferiority complex about being daytime. Daytime stars are seldom asked on talk shows or even game shows. They usually only get bit parts in nighttime drama. I was the only daytime star who'd ever had my own evening special.

Mama tossed the quartered chicken into a large casserole. "I didn't tell Bernadette you're leaving the show, because we must tell Fedora first."

"Mama, what does he want?"

"He wants to talk about doing a book. Don't you love it? He's only going to be at The Plaza for twenty-four hours. Some notice. Twenty-four hours with Labor Day weekend coming up!"

"A book about me?"

"Not a book about me," Mama said.

"Oh, Mama!"

"Don't oh Mama me. This is your vacation, and after it, you're going to college. Remember?"

"But I could talk with him, couldn't I?"

"If he still wants to talk with you after he finds out you're leaving the show, then he can come back to New York."

"We could go in tonight, Mama," I said.

"You've got a date tonight."

"With Wally, Mama. Just with Wally."

"And I'm fixing Charlie a complete Spanish dinner which I'm now in the process of preparing."

"We could drive into New York very late. We'd avoid traffic."

Mama said, "I'm not going to cook a complete Spanish dinner and then haul my ass into New York because some big-shot writer had a lightbulb go on in his head while he's sipping martinis over the Atlantic. If he still wants to do the story after he learns you're leaving *Hometown*, he can fly his butt back and set up an appointment with you!"

Mama took out the chopping block and banged an onion down on it.

"Any other time you'd jump at the chance," I said.

"*You'd* jump at the chance, Maggie," said Mama. "You got your ulcer jumping at chances in case anyone should ride up on a bicycle and ask you!"

I picked up the tray she'd fixed for me. "What letter was Bernadette talking about?" I asked.

"A personal letter," Mama said. "Am I allowed a personal letter?"

I left Mama in the kitchen hacking an onion to pieces and took the tray up to my room. I blow-dried my hair and tried to put together something to wear, while I munched on the chicken.

The sandals I'd worn to The Surf Club were the only shoes I'd brought out that I could dance in; they didn't go with jeans. What would go with my jeans were shoes I'd used on the show, but I couldn't dance in them. All the shoes we wore in the show had rubber on the bottoms, a fluted kind of rubber that kept us from slipping on stage. Most of them were nude colored so they didn't draw attention to our feet.

I was pulling hangers out and opening drawers for a long time. I heard Charlie come back from his swim, and Charlie and Mama laughing. I finally decided there was no way I could go to that party and look or act like Nancy Normal, so I went the other way. I wore my nude-colored shoes with the rubber soles, jeans and a TELL ME MORE T-shirt. I carried my blue zippered jacket with HOMETOWN lettered on it, and my blue canvas bag with HOMETOWN stitched across it. We wore a lot of that kind of thing on the set, while we were rehearsing.

Just before the taxi pulled in with Wally, I went downstairs and sneaked into Mama's bedroom. There was a pile of mail on her dressing table, bills mostly; I sifted through them. The letter from Bernadette Young was on the bottom.

Dear Peg,

Lamont has this feeling he can't work with Fedora or Sabra because of your antagonism. I quote: "Ever since our meeting at

The New School, Peg seemed for me. We had a good relationship, as you know. She told me about the opening for writers on Hometown and encouraged me to try out. But after I started with the show, she changed. It's Sabra, of course; it always is. Peg imagines she's protecting Sabra (from heaven knows what!) but the truth is Sabra controls Peg in a very insidious way. Peg could never tell her about us, and she discarded me the same way she did Nick: 'for Sabra's sake.' Then Peg got it into her head that Sabra was attracted to me, or I was to her. Now she just wants me out. . . . I want this job, Bernadette, but I'm caught between these two females: one, a lonely, lovely lady who won't let her daughter grow up and take her own chances; the other, a self-absorbed child who lives in the fantasy of her own storylines, and won't let her mother go."

These are harsh words, maybe, Peg but we've known each other for a long time. I think there's some truth to what Lamont says, and I hope when you meet with him in Seaville, you'll view him more objectively, and also keep my confidence re: the above.

Lamont does deserve the job. Pigheaded as he is, he's the best writer for what Fedora has in mind. Think about it.

Love,
Berna

17. Wallace Witherspoon, Jr.

When I got there, Charlie and Mrs. St. Amour were sitting on the sun porch drinking sangria. Sabra had her bag under her arm and seemed eager to go. I asked her to open up the package I had with me, first.

She pulled out the T-shirt and held it up.

"Grab the Reins!" Charlie said. "That's what your shrink said to you."

"That's what her shrink on the show said to her," Mrs. St. Amour said. "That's not what her own shrink said to her ever. Her own shrink says hello and goodbye and very little in between, which we pay her fifty dollars an hour for!"

"Was it the shrink on *Hometown*?" I said.

Mrs. St. Amour said, "Yes, Dr. Day, played by Paula Willow."

"My own shrink said something very similar, if not those very words," said Sabra.

"When?" Mrs. St. Amour asked.

'Sabra ignored her mother's question and glanced over at me. "Thanks a lot, Wally. Shall we go?"

" 'Grab the reins' was Lamont's line in case anyone is interested," said Mrs. St. Amour. "I know everything he ever wrote for *Hometown*."

"And you always called it garbage," said Sabra.

"Well you remember garbage," Mrs. St. Amour said,

laughing, "Lamont wrote it."

"It doesn't matter who said it," Charlie said. "It's still a good line."

"It's *good* garbage, hah?" Mrs. St. Amour laughed again.

Sabra wasn't even smiling.

I said, "I guess you're not going to Deke's party, Charlie."

"We're going to have a complete Spanish dinner," Charlie said. "Just Mrs. St. Amour and me."

"You can call me Peg, Charlie," said Mrs. St. Amour. "You can, too, Wally."

"I don't think I'd have a great time at Deke Slade's house anyway," Charlie said.

Mrs. St. Amour said, "Oh is that why I've been cutting up chickens and chopping onions and frying sausages and steaming mussels, because you don't think you'd have a great time someplace else?" She mussed up Charlie's hair and went back to the kitchen.

"Hey, don't go away mad, Peg," Charlie called after her.

Sabra let out a long, exasperated sigh and snatched the car keys from the table. "Ready, Wally?"

"Grab the reins," I said.

"Okay, you made your point."

"What does that mean: I made my point?"

"Nothing," she said. "I just hope you're not going to say that all night long."

For a while, I didn't think I was going to get to say anything all night long. On the way to Deke's, she kept up this running monologue about some writer who wanted to do a book about her.

"Did you ever hear the name Milton Tanner?"

"Who's he?"

"Who's he," she said sarcastically.

"Well tell me who he is, if he's someone."

"Skip it," she said. "Will there be a lot of people at this party?" She had her foot down on the gas pedal; we were clocking eighty-five.

"If we live to get there," I said.

I was getting a little steamed. I kept thinking that Harriet or Lauralei would have put on any T-shirt I'd bought them, immediately, and worn it to the party. Sabra was wearing one with her own picture on it, carrying a jacket and a bag with her show's name on them. It was hard to get her attention, too.

When I said, "I've been thinking of going to college in New York City—N.Y.U. or Columbia," she said, "Nobody in daytime has ever had a whole book written about her."

"Of course it's a year away," I said.

"The first book Milton Tanner wrote was about Marilyn Monroe."

"Anyway, I'm not going to follow in my father's footsteps. That's all settled."

"He wrote one about James Dean, too," said Sabra.

Deke's party was in an old, cleared-out greenhouse behind the Slades' house. Mr. Slade was expanding to the lot next door, where the new greenhouse was and his nursery. Sabra had to park the Mercedes about ten doors away, there were so many cars on the block already. We could hear a Captain & Tennille record blasting while we were still locking the car.

Deke always stocked up on French cigarettes when he gave a party. He passed them around in case someone from his family wandered in and smelled the pot. Deke would hold up a Gauloise and say, "This is what smells."

"Yiiiiik, grass!" Sabra said when we walked inside. "I hate that smell!"

"I thought you lived a sheltered life."

"*I* do," she said. "We had an actor who'd get so laid back on grass we had to stop the tape for him every time he tried to say his lines."

"It gives me a headache," I said. I'd only had it once, with Lauralei Rabinowitz. I felt as thought an ax was impaled somewhere between my ears, and Lauralei kept whispering, "Are you flying?" ("No, but if *you* are, fly down to the drugstore and get me some Anacin," I said.)

Deke Slade came rushing up to us. "You must be Sabra St. Amour."

"Tell me more!" someone sang out.

Sabra's face brightened. "Here we go," she said. "Fasten your seat belt, Wally."

At first there was this huge fuss over her. Duffo Buttman asked her for her autograph again; he said there were butter stains all over the lobster bib she'd signed for him. Some of the other kids came by to be introduced, and she signed the cast on Linda Crawford's leg which Linda had broken falling out of Eddie Gallagher's speedboat. Sandy Rapp, Seaville High's favorite drama department star, asked Sabra how to get an agent, and Annie Butler, Seaville High's aspiring television director, asked her a question about unions. There was the usual autographing and barefaced gawking.

I got a beer for myself and a ginger ale for Sabra. When I started back toward her, I saw something beginning to happen. I heard it, too. There was this peculiar voice change, almost as though she was doing a parody of herself. She was talking very slowly, pronouncing every word very exactly, in this high, stilted tone. She would emphasize some of the things she said by closing her eyes for a moment, as though she was punctuating that way. I got a little closer to her, and I heard her say, ". . . and I told him, 'Accept me as I am, so I may learn what I can become.'"

I recognized the line from the poster Sabra on *Hometown* tacked on her wall when she arrived in Clear City. Maybe some of the other kids did, too, or maybe it was just the way she was coming off, like she was on a little ego trip all her own. She didn't hear the snickers in the background. Her eyes were closed for a moment. She heard Myra Tuttle, who was standing in front of her say, "What a neat answer!" and Duffo Buttman's "Hey!"

But kids were beginning to exchange looks, you know the kind of looks I mean: the get *her* ones, and the ones of suppressed laughter with the hands cupping the mouths.

There was still a crowd around her when a familiar perfume got through the pot fumes, and I heard the low chuckle, and my own name, softly.

I turned and looked up at Lauralei Rabinowitz with Maury Posner.

It was a scene from my richest fantasies: There I was with a superstar, there Lauralei was still with Maury Posner. But it was not turning out exactly as I'd seen it in my imagination, because a flood of intense, warm feelings for Lauralei Rabinowitz rushed past and smothered my victory, and I was beginning to worry about Sabra.

"Did you bring Lauralei that beer?" said Maury, reaching down and taking the can from my hand.

"He didn't bring me that beer, I bet," Lauralei said.

"You can have that beer," I said.

Maury began drinking it, while I stood looking up at her, trying to fight off all the old symptoms of Rabinowitzitis. She leaned over to talk to me.

"I guess you don't think about me anymore," she purred.

"I think about you."

"Not anymore, I bet."

I glanced in Sabra's direction. She was holding forth but no longer holding anyone's full attention. The looks were beginning to spread.

"I want to tell you something," Lauralei Rabinowitz said.

"Can you tell me later?"

She gave me one of her smiles. "Can I tell you now?" She stuck one of her long fingers through the belt loop on my jeans. "Please?"

"Certainly," I said. "Absolutely," I added.

She leaned down even closer to me. "Hey," she whispered.

"Hey what?" I answered weakly, trying to keep an eye on Sabra, sinking a little more every second into my old disease. Lauralei's soft, long black hair brushed my forehead.

"Hey how come you brought a pain-in-the-ass to the party," she said, "and how come your breath smells of onions?"

On my way back to Sabra, I slipped a Tic Tac in my mouth and grabbed another can of beer from the pail of ice. Where was kindness in the world? I wondered, where was consideration, respect, goodness? I remembered a line from a Woody Allen book when the hero asked a girl where reality was and she said it was north. *No, Harriet. Empty dreams are north. Reality is west. False hope are east, and I think Louisiana is south.*

I wanted to get Sabra away from the small crowd still

hanging around her. Some of them were beginning to laugh openly; others were feeding her lines. I don't think she got what was happening, but she sensed something was in the air. I took her off to the side and said, "They're dancing out on the deck. Do you want to dance?"

"I don't have the right shoes," she said.

I handed her the ginger ale. A few people still drifted by and stared at her and there were several "Tell me mores" tossed out, but after a while everyone was too stoned to move, or too busy dancing, or too into their own things. We stood there.

"So this is normal," she said. "They might as well all be from Mars."

"They don't know how to talk to you," I said.

"*They* don't know how to talk to *me*?" She gave a loud guffaw.

"You were sort of doing a number, too."

"I was what?"

"Doing a number. Talking the way you talk on the show."

"The writers write the way *I* talk," she said. "I don't talk the way the writers write." She shook her head as though she was amazed she had to explain anything that simple to anyone.

"Is that the way you talk to the kids you go to school with?"

"We don't socialize a lot," she said. "We don't have time for this—" She waved her hand as though she was waving away flying cockroaches, and didn't finish the sentence.

"Just what did you expect?" I asked her.

"Just where is the john?" she answered.

I chug-a-lugged two cans of beer waiting for her. I watched her walk back from the john alone. No one was paying any attention to her anymore, not even laughing at her behind her back. I felt almost the way I felt sometimes at school, when Charlie was standing around in a group of us. Whoever'd talk would meet everyone's eye but his, and I'd want to say Jesus, look at Charlie, too, he's standing right here with us. . . . It wasn't quite like that because what everybody at Deke's was doing finally was forgetting all about her, that she was even there, and going on with their own business.

I looked at her in the T-shirt with her picture on it, in the jacket with the name of the show on it, carrying the *Hometown* bag, and inside the "Tell me more" ball-point pen to sign autographs with, and I remembered how she'd bragged about the man who wanted to write a book about her. She was looking all around her, as though she couldn't believe she wasn't being watched. I told myself I'd take her down to the ocean. I'd tell her the Queen of England could walk through one of Deke's parties with a cortege of naked noblemen and no one would even turn around, once they were all freaked out on pot. I'd pick up a six-pack and take her somewhere and ask her all about herself and listen to her and feature her.

"Let's split," I said as she walked up to me.

"Let's."

I grabbed her hand. "C'mon!"

When she started the car, I said, "I know somewhere we can pick up some beer."

She reached down and slapped in a tape, turning up Frank Sinatra full pitch singing "Violets for Your Furs."

"Mama loves this song," she said. "She knows all the words."

She drove down Main Street going slowly, for her, around forty.

"We can pick up some beer at The Deli-Mavin," I said. "It's on the left."

"Is that what you want, beer?" she said.

"Yes," I said.

"Is that what you're going to drink on your way to New York?" she said.

She didn't stop at The Deli-Mavin. She kept right on going, and it wasn't until we were on the Montauk Highway that I realized there were tears streaming down her face.

18. Sabra St. Amour

I remember when this character in *Hometown* went crazy after she was gang-raped by The Motorcycle Satyrs. She got into her Volkswagen and drove down to the main street in Pine Bluff, rolled up the windows, locked the doors, put her hand on the horn and screamed.

The writer told Fedora he got the idea for the scene from an old Dory Previn record, about a woman who began screaming in a twenty-mile zone. The song was supposed to be based on something Dory Previn did during a nervous breakdown.

I was thinking about that while I drove Wally into New York; I was thinking that I didn't want to go crazy on the Montauk Highway. If I was going to crack up, I'd hold it in until I hit the city. If you have to blow your cork, New York City is the ideal place, maybe the only place you can walk around totally insane and still not be conspicuous.

I was also trying to tell myself it was possible it'd pass, the way Etta Lott's hysteria did the night the powerful mayor threatened to force her into an abortion. Etta Lott had pulled herself together by telling herself she was made of stronger fiber than that. She'd sat down with an old picture album of her family for generations back, and watched their faces, and drummed it into herself that the Lotts were survivors. Well that was one way I was not going to be able to get myself off the hook, because we didn't even own a camera until The Dark Ages, and old pictures of Sam, Sam, Superman would only push me all the way around the bend.

I think Wally was afraid we'd be traffic-accident statistics before we left Suffolk County, even though I was taking it easy for me. In Bridgehampton I stopped so he could buy humself a six-pack, and me some Merits. He didn't give me his usual spiel about smoking; he hardly touched the beer.

I knew he was afraid to chance any loss of control, because he sensed I was on the verge of losing all control.

I stopped crying just before we reached Bridgehampton. When Wally lighted a Merit for me, I sucked the smoke deep into my lungs and let it narcotize me ("He's narcotized now," a police detective said once on *Hometown*, after letting this heroin addict shoot up in his cell. "We'll be able to get more out of him now.") I turned off the tape.

I began to talk. I told Wally everything that had happened between Mama and me: all about Lamont, and Nick before Lamont, about Bernadette's letter and the lies Mama'd told me. It was a nice talk, in a way, a strange, peaceful talk, as though we were simply two old friends going for a drive somewhere, filling in the time with conversation.

I remember at one point Wally said quietly, "But you know, it sounds like you were doing to your mother what my father was doing to me."

"What do you mean?" I asked him, and I was calm, too.

"You were forcing your life on her, the way he was forcing his on me."

"I don't think you're listening," I said, because I couldn't see that at all, and he said, "Oh I'm listening, Sabra. Honestly.

Go on," humoring me, probably sorry he'd ventured an opinion.

I said, "Mama was the one who always told me I wasn't just another salami on the deli ceiling."

"That's a good way to put it," Wally said. He wasn't going to risk any more.

I said, "Mama's always talking about getting out of the business, but we all talk that way." I laughed. "Then in the next breath she asks Fedora for five hundred more clams a month."

"Yeah," Wally agreed.

"You see it's in our blood," I said.

"Right," Wally said.

"Mama just has a weakness for weak men," I said.

"I see."

"Mama has a weakness for weakness." I laughed.

Wally laughed, too.

"Don't humor me," I said.

"Who's humoring you?"

"Don't throw bouquets at me," I said. "Don't laugh at my jokes too much. Do you know that old song?

"I don't think so."

"It's called 'People Will Say We're in Love.' It was Mama's song with Sam, Sam, Superman, my stepfather."

"Why did you call him that?" Wally said.

"It was Mama's name for him," I said. "Mama used to tell him he could do anything she set her mind to." I remembered the time back in The Dark Ages when T.V. commercials first began featuring men and women who didn't look like models or movie stars. The casting directors called them "uglies." One night at dinner, after Mama'd splurged on a bottle of twenty-five-dollar champagne, she talked Sam, Sam into answering a casting call for an actor to play a bartender. He was supposed to hold up a bottle of new light beer called Pebble and say, "Pebble promises pleasure."

Sam, Sam kept saying it was a tongue twister, and he'd end up saying "Plebble plomises pleasure" when he'd practice with Mama. Mama got him to say "Peggy Babcock" fast, over and over, so he'd master tongue twisting. "If you can say 'Peggy Babcock' five times fast, you can say anything," Mama'd tell him.

We both went in with Sam, Sam when he had his appointment at the agency. The casting director raised her eyebrow with pleasure when she saw him, looked over his shoulder at Mama and shook her head up and down. (He was an ugly, all right.) When it came Sam's turn to try out, he held up the bottle and said, "Peggy Babcock, Peggy Babcock."

I just groaned and turned my back because it hurt to look, but Mama went tearing up to the set and threw her arms around him, and they both collapsed with laughter.

P.S. He didn't get the part.

P.P.S. He always used it later in arguments, as an example of Mama pushing him.

I told Wally about that and about a lot of other things. I thought of what they say about someone drowning, that your whole life passes before your eyes while you're waterlogged and going under.

Usually when I see the lights of Manhattan, on the way in, I breathe a sigh of relief, the way people do when they see the Statue of Liberty in New York Harbor on their way back from Europe, and know they're home. All the lights and the bridges and the tall buildings in the shadows always tranquilized me.

That night, though, I could feel something revving up inside me because we were almost there, and then what?

Once the door shut behind us in the apartment at The Dakota, I could feel Wally tense up, too.

"It's eleven forty-five, Sabra," he said. "This is no time to call a writer."

"Have a beer," I said, and I looked up the number of The Plaza in the Manhattan telephone directory.

"We ought to call and tell people where we are," he said.

"We will," I said, "*after*."

"Sabra, he's going to think you're—"

"*What?*" I said.

"Nothing," he said. "It's just the wrong thing to do."

"Have a beer," I said. "Relax. How do you like our place?"

"I wish you'd wait until tomorrow," said Wally.

"I can't wait until tomorrow," I said.

"Why?" he said.

"Necessity relieves us from the embarrassment of choice," I said.

"Now that's a line from the show," he said. "Isn't that some line from the show?"

"So what?" I said.

"So you're doing a number again," he said. "Why can't you just come up with a normal answer?"

"Like what?" I said.

"Huh?"

"What's a normal answer for why I'm about to call Milton Tanner?"

"Jesus!" he said.

"Because I'll be happy to come up with it if you'll tell me what it is."

"Oh God," he said.

"Then you'll love me because I'll be more like you," I said.

"You don't want anyone to love you in the ninth place," he said.

"No, I want to call Milton Tanner," I said.

It was almost midnight by the time I reached him. I explained who I was and that I was ready to do the interview anytime, and Wally stood across from me punching his forehead with his fist and making faces.

"I'm sorry it's so late," I said.

"I'm an insomniac, anyway," he said. "What's your address?"

"Are you humoring me, too?" I said. Wally shut his eyes and grimaced.

"Am I humoring you?" Milton Tanner said.

"Yes," I said.

"Yeah, I'm humoring you," he said. "I'll see you in twenty minutes."

Next I called Mama.

"Well isn't that just ducky," Mama said. "That's just ducky that you called Milton Tanner. Be sure and make him right at home. Is Wally with you?"

"Why did you lie, Mama?" I said.

"I asked you if Wally was with you?"

"He's with me," I said. "You could have told me you met

Lamont at The New School."

"You tell Wally his mother's looking for him," she said. "You hear?"

"All those lies, Mama. All the times you laughed at Lamont with me and you were—" I couldn't even say it. "With him."

"The next time you read my mail, put it back in order. Try to have a little mystery about you, Maggie. Is your stomach all right?"

"The way you have mystery about you?" I said.

"Maybe I should have told you but as it turned out I didn't," Mama said.

"And that's all you're going to say?"

"No, that isn't all I'm going to say, but it's all I'm going to say *ce soir*, Maggie, because I've got a load of dishes to do and I've had it with you just taking off when you feel like it!"

"Just one lie after the other," I said.

"You never liked anyone I picked," Mama said.

"Maybe because your taste is terrible."

"It's the one thing that's all mine, though, Maggie." I didn't say anything. I could feel things beginning to crumble inside, as though instead of internal organs there was a house of cards under my skin, and the top card had slipped.

"Tell Wally to call home," Mama said, "and call me in the morning. You're on your own now, Maggie."

"Wait," I said, but I heard the click, then the dial tone.

I was still in my bedroom staring at the Will Barnet print over my bed when I heard the doorbell, and then Wally talking to someone. Mama and I have a lot of Will Barnet prints and there are always cats in them. I remembered a cat

I had once back in The Dark Ages, a tabby I called Loser, because he always positioned himself under this birdhouse that was on top of a long iron pole. There was no way he could ever catch a bird from that birdhouse, but he never tried another position, and he wouldn't even come in out of the rain once he stationed himself there afternoons.

Sam, Sam used to holler at me, "You better get that word 'loser' out of your vocabulary, baby doll! You and your mother use that word about other people a little too much! There's such a thing as winning and losing, but there's no such thing as winners and losers. We all take turns at it. You'll see, someday."

I glanced up at the ceiling. "Okay, Sam, Sam," I said.

I got up from my bed and went toward the living room. I could hear Wally saying softly, " . . . not herself, so you'll have to—"

"Have to what?" I said from the doorway. "Have to what?"

"Hi, I'm Milton Tanner." He looked a lot like Telly Savalas, tall and bald, with green-tinted lenses in silver frames. He had his hand out.

We shook.

"Now where can have some privacy?" he said.

"In my bedroom?" I said.

Wally was slumped on the couch, holding a can of beer.

"Lead the way," Milton Tanner said.

He sat down on my chaise lounge, kicked off his loafers and put his feet up.

"Do you have a tape recorder on you?" I said.

"No, I don't use one."

"Because I don't want to talk into one," I said.

"I don't use a tape recorder."

I stood there, and he sat there, and we both seemed to be waiting.

Then I sat on the chair in front of my dressing table and said, "There are some rumors that I'm leaving the show but I'm not."

"Okay," he said. He looked at me, waiting again.

I said, "Mr. Tanner?"

"You can call me Milton."

"Milton?"

"What?"

"I had a fight with my mother. I found something out."

"Well?"

"Well listen, I'd better tell you something first."

"What's that?"

"I think I'm going crazy."

"No you're not," he said.

"Yes, I think I am, Mr. Tanner, and I mean that."

"You're not going crazy, Sabra," he said. "You already are. You always have been. You have to be in this business. This is a business for crazy people, see."

"I believe my own storyline."

"You better believe it, you wouldn't be any damn good if you didn't."

"I say things some writer wrote for me instead of what I feel."

"Neither does anyone, really. Neither does an audience. You and the writer tell them what they feel."

"I don't think I'm getting through to you," I said.

"You're coming in loud and clear, Sabra," he said. "Now that kid out there in the other room isn't crazy. He's some nice kid who's worried about you, but he needn't be. Someday something you'll say, or someone like you will say, will stick in his head, and he might even act on it, be better for it, but he'll never be able to show it to someone else quite the way you showed it to him. You know why?"

"Why?"

"Normal people are self-conscious. They can't act out. They wait for someone mad to interpret what they feel, someone who'll step forward and say The hell with how this looks to other people, I'm going to show you yourself and myself and him and her, watch me! Now only a crazy risks that because you can wind up with egg on your face."

"Etta Lott, on *Hometown*, said you have to step out of line to give the world something special," I told him.

"Oh yeah, way out of line. . . . Daisy Harrow played Etta, didn't she?"

"I was trying to remember her name just this afternoon."

"She got a part in a series," he said, "something Gene Reynolds is putting together for CBS. Honey, can we shut off your phone? In about ten minutes I'm going to be bothered with calls from the coast. I left this number like a damn fool."

"Someday I'd like to do a series," I said, switching off the phone.

"Someday you will," he said. "Where were you born, anyway?"

"New Hope, Pennsylvania," I said. "Mama and my dad were doing a show up there that summer."

"Sure, at the Bucks County Playhouse."

"That's right," I said.

He took out a pack of Camels and offered one to me. I

reached for it saying, "I shouldn't. I have an ulcer."

"Then don't," he said, putting the pack away. "I had one of those once. They go away. . . . Was your mother acting that summer at Bucks?"

"Was she ever! I was practically born on stage. That's quite a story in itself," I began.

19. Wallace Witherspoon, Jr.

On the first day of my last year at Seaville High, there was a funeral for Priscilla Sigh, only survivor and sister of Mr. Sigh; he died the night I was in New York with Sabra.

Instead of going to the school cafeteria for lunch, I went home to help Charlie, who was in charge of the services and burial.

While Charlie was mingling with the bereaved in our chapel, I grabbed a peanut-butter sandwich in the kitchen.

"At least poor Prissy didn't linger on long after she lost him," my mother was saying as she fixed herself a salad.

"Do we *have* to live with that thing?" I asked her, pointing to the cornucopia on the top of our refrigerator.

"Charlie's mother brought that over today," my mother said, "and yes, we have to live with it, if Charlie wants it. I rather like it, and I want Charlie to feel right at home here."

We could hear the strains of "Abide With Me" as Mr. Llewellyn played the organ in the chapel. My father was on his way to the Hauppauge morgue to pick up our new guest, a Mrs. Fabray. A.E. was in school.

Mr. Trumble was still in Southampton Hospital, recovering slowly from a heart attack he'd had the same night Mr. Sigh died.

I often wonder what would have happened if Milton Tanner hadn't shut off the phone that night, and my mother had been able to reach me. I only know what wouldn't have happened. Charlie wouldn't have offered to help out, and my father wouldn't have gotten the idea to ask Charlie to come into the business with him.

Things can change overnight…or as Monty Montgomery had put it a few days ago at Current Events: "Chance makes a football of man's life, Withered Heart. … A woman has *everything*: a good man, a good home, a faithful dog, and chance blows a lathe operator from Commack her way— and she gives it all up! For *what*?"

"I don't know," I said. "Maybe she needed a change."

"A change from what?" he said. "She had the world on a string. . . . Oh, I'll get along all right. Lunch and I'll get along all right, won't we, fellow?"

The dog looked up at him from the floor and opened his good eye, then rested his head on his paws and sighed.

"It's Martha who's in for it," Monty said, "and I blame all this women's liberation crap she came across in all these ladies' magazines."

I reached for a radish from my mother's salad and she said, "Don't, Wally. Your father always says radishes are just as strong on the breath as onions. You'll have to help Charlie with the bereaved. It's his maiden voyage, after all."

I washed my sandwich down with a glass of milk and went down the hall toward our chapel. Charlie was standing just outside, in the alcove, talking on the telephone. He was wearing a new blue suit, white shirt, and dark blue tie. He was wearing the gold tie clasp with the crown on it that he'd won in the dance contest Labor Day weekend. Mrs. St. Amour and Charlie took first prize doing an old dance called the Lambeth Walk.

Sabra never returned to Seaville. The last time I saw her was when I woke up on her couch in their apartment. It was around ten in the morning and she was fixing a pot of coffee for Milton Tanner. I got on the phone and called the Long Island Railroad to find out what time I could get a train back to Seaville.

"We talked all night," she told me. "I'm sorry if I worried you, Wally, but Milton says a chaotic temperament is a natural to an actress."

"I don't have any quarrel with that," I said. "Goodbye, Sabra."

"Never say good-bye," she said, taking my hand, closing her eyes for a moment, opening them and looking deeply into mine. "We'll meet again in another time, in another place, who knows when? But until we do it's not good-bye, not for you and me ever. Say it isn't."

"It isn't," I said.

"Take long steps and by all means look back," she said. "You'll see everything behind you getting smaller, and eventually passing completely out of view."

"Nice," I said. "Who wrote it?"

Sabra laughed. "Who cares?" she said. "*I* said it."

Yesterday when my mother came home from Mr. Jim's Beauty Parlor, she had this clipping she'd torn out of *The Examiner*, from a gossip column on soap operas:

> From "Hometown" comes news that young Sabra St. Amour will have a registered nurse in attendance while she is on the set, due to a precarious health problem she is doing her best to lick. Her fans will be pulling for her,

as she makes a heroic effort to go on with the show. . . . Meanwhile, "Mama's" being seen around town with a certain bigwig writer from the coast, who's rumored to be doing a book about Sabra. Good luck to all of them!

I stood beside Charlie, waiting for him to get off the phone, holding my watch under his nose to remind him the services were due to begin at twelve thirty.

"I don't have anything against you, personally, Deke," Charlie was saying. "The Sigh funeral flowers came from Pittman Florists, that's all."

I whispered, "It's twelve forty. I have to be back by one."

"I don't know who'll get the order for the Fabray flowers," said Charlie. "I leave that up to the bereaved. . . . See you around, buddy."

Then Charlie hung up. "I'll be a son of BEAMS," he said, "Deke actually begged me to remember we were old friends."

In the chapel, Charlie and I helped the mourners to their seats, and then before Reverend Monroe began the eulogy and prayers, Charlie made a little speech about the Sighs' importance to Seaville. He stood at the lectern and talked to the gathering as though he's been doing it all his life. One old lady even clapped when Charlie finished.

Reverend Monroe took me aside at the end of the service, while Charlie went up to close the casket. The mourners filed out to the waiting limousines, and the pallbearers stood in readiness just outside the chapel door.

"What a blessing Charlie's going to be to your father," said Reverend Monroe. "Are you accompanying us to the cemetery, Wally?"

"I have to go back to school," I said. "Charlie will handle it."

"He certainly will!" said Reverend Monroe enthusiastically.

At a signal from Charlie, the pallbearers filed in to lift the coffin.

It was then that we heard it, a sudden, incredible, inhuman sound, an eerie moaning going higher and higher: Arrrrrrrrrrrr-ow, Arrrrrrrrrrrrr-ow!

The pallbearers jumped back.

Reverend Monroe and I rushed into the chapel.

Charlie opened the coffin and Gorilla leaped out and rushed past us with her hair standing up and her tail flagging.

"Shall we proceed?" Charlie asked everyone.

My first glimpse of Lauralei Rabinowitz, on my first day of my last year at Seaville High, came after last class. She was walking by herself out the front door, and I caught up with her. It was a fine fall afternoon with the leaves turning and drifting down lazily from the trees, and Lauralei Rabinowitz looked down at me with a sweet smile.

"Hi," I said.

"Hi, Wally."

"Where's Maury?"

"Maury who?" she said, tossing back her long, soft, black hair, grinning into my eyes.

"*Oh*," I said.

"Yes, *oh*," she said. "That's *fini, chéri*."

I felt a sudden, lovely glow, as though maybe this new

school year was going to be the best one, and it was senior year, too: the last, the best.

"How have *you* been, Wally?" she said in her breathless tone.

"Just great," I said. "Have you heard the news about me?"

"What's the news about you?" she said, hooking her arm in mine, brushing against me while we went down the winding walk from school.

"I'm not going to be an undertaker," I said.

"Marvelous!" she said. "Super! . . . Now if you were two feet taller and your name was Witherstein, you'd be perfect!"

Well, as my Uncle Albert is fond of saying, you can't win them all.

THE END

Other Titles You Will Enjoy
From Lizzie Skurnick Books

TO ALL MY FANS, WITH LOVE, FROM SYLVIE by Ellen Conford. Ellen Conford's classic 1982 road novel takes place over the course of five days as we follow the comic misadventures of fifteen-year-old Sylvie.

SECRET LIVES by Berthe Amoss. Set against the backdrop of 1930s New Orleans, Berthe Amoss's 1979 young adult mystery follows twelve-year-old Addie Agnew as she struggles to uncover the secret of her mother's death.

HAPPY ENDINGS ARE ALL ALIKE by Sandra Scoppetone. At a time when girls were only allowed to date boys, Jaret and Peggy know they had to keep their love a secret.

A LONG DAY IN NOVEMBER by Ernest Gaines. Told from the perspective of a six-year old boy, this unforgettable story leads the reader through an eventful day on a Southern sugarcane plantation in the 1940s.

WRITTEN IN THE STARS: Early Stories by Lois Duncan. From the master of thrillers and the supernatural comes a collection of her earliest stories that have never been published before in book form.

Subscribe to Lizzie Skurnick Books and receive a book a month delivered right to your front door. Online at **http://igpub.com/lizzie-skurnick-books-subscription/**